DATE DUE

JUL 2 7 2005	

*Just Some Weeds
from the Wilderness*

Just Some Weeds from the Wilderness

Patricia Beatty

BOOKSALE

William Morrow and Company
New York   1978

Library of Congress Cataloging in Publication Data
Beatty, Patricia
Just some weeds from the wilderness.
Summary: In an attempt to change the family's
failing fortune, Lucinda's aunt goes into
the business of producing a patent medicine.
[1. Oregon—Fiction]   I. Title.
PZ7.B380544Ju   [Fic]   77-28433
ISBN 0-688-22137-8   ISBN 0-688-32137-2 lib. bdg.

Printed in the United States of America.
First Edition
1   2   3   4   5   6   7   8   9   10

To my friends and fellow-writers,
Dorothy Leon and Lael Littke

Contents

Just Some Weeds
from the Wilderness

CHAPTER I

"We Are Ruined, My Dears!"

I'll never forget that very strange New Year's Eve of 1873.

It wasn't only that this was the year that I turned thirteen and so believed that I should be allowed to stay up till midnight and have some dandelion wine with Mama, Aunt Adelina, and Uncle Silas Westlake. No, I will always remember it for another reason. It was the New Year's Eve that Aunt Adelina did a startling thing and said an even more startling one.

To begin with, she didn't play "Auld Lang Syne" on the cottage organ, to see the old year out in a proper manner, the way she had for as long as I could remember. Instead she banged out "Onward Christian Soldiers," which my brother, Henry Frederick, and I thought was a very peculiar tune for the occasion. Oh, we sang it along with her and so did Mama and Uncle Silas, but all the same we wondered why we weren't getting "Auld Lang Syne," which went with New Year's Eve the way ham went with eggs.

After the hymn was over, Aunt Adelina got straight up from the organ and went over to the heavy golden-oak table, set in the middle of our parlor. Standing up as tall as she could, which made her very close to five feet high, she picked up a glass of the shining, yellow wine she made every year from dandelion heads. She told her husband, Silas, "Please fill Lucinda's thimble and give it to her." Her sharp, dark eyes were fixed on my face, and she wasn't smiling. "Lucinda, you said that you only wanted a thimbleful of wine tonight, though I suspect you hoped for more. Well, let this be a lesson to you. People are far more likely to get what they ask for when they aren't coy about it. Your mother would never have permitted you to have a full glass of dandelion wine, but half a glass would have been a different matter."

"Yes, ma'am," was what I said, as I took the silver thimble from Uncle Silas's pudgy fingers. It was tarnished, and I guessed that Mrs. Apley, who cleaned for us, had overlooked it in my aunt's embroidery basket when she polished the rest of the silver. While I waited for Mama to pick up her wineglass and for Uncle Silas to say what he always said for the New Year, "Bottoms up!" followed by a funny little speech, I looked around the parlor at my family.

Only five of us lived in the big white house in Denton, Oregon. There were we three Howards, Mama, Henry Frederick, who was eleven, and myself, Lucinda Lavina.

My brother was sulking at that moment because he was too young for even a thimbleful of wine. And then there were the two Westlakes, Uncle Silas and Aunt Adelina.

People said that Henry Frederick and I looked alike. We were both medium-statured for our ages, blue-eyed, pale-skinned, and on the way to becoming brunet from having been blond. I didn't relish looking like him any more than he relished looking like me. And secretly I hoped his nose would turn out different from mine so we'd look less alike from now on.

Mama, a widow, was Aunt Adelina's sister. She was dark-haired like Adelina but taller by a couple inches. Tonight Mama looked melancholy in her black-trimmed, lavender-velvet mourning gown. Before Aunt Adelina had played "Onward Christian Soldiers" and come out with her startling remark, I'd reckoned that Mama was sad because this New Year's Eve of 1873 probably made her think of our father, who had been killed in battle in 1864, the next-to-last year of the dreadful Civil War. Ten years ago she and Papa had enjoyed their last New Year's Eve together back home in Pennsylvania.

I glanced from her to my uncle, who was dressed in black and white as always. It seemed to me that his blond beard looked straggly tonight. He was very proud of it and was always shaping and trimming it, along with his curling side-burns. What I could see of his face above his beard didn't look so good tonight either. It was a sort of grayish color, which wasn't natural for such a pink-skinned man.

Aunt Adelina, standing beside him, had bright spots on her cheeks, not garnet red like her second-best silk dress, of course, because nobody's cheeks ever got that color unless they had chilblains. But the red wasn't the color a lady got from wet red flannel either. She was plenty angry about something. It seemed to me that she was quivering all over, from the tortoiseshell comb stuck in her piled-up, gray curls down to her kid-leather boots. Those almond-shaped, dark eyes of hers were glittering. Yes, sir, either someone had done something she didn't like or something had happened that she didn't like.

I supposed it was Uncle Silas. He certainly looked pretty sheepish about something. Sneaking another glance at his face I knew that it was. What's more he didn't say his usual "Bottoms up!" at all.

Before he could say anything Aunt Adelina put in, "Silas, I think this year *I* shall make the toast to the New Year. Perhaps my doing so will change our luck. All right, here is to 1874! May it be a better year than this last one has been."

When she put her glass to her lips I tossed off my wine in one gulp, which was very easy to do from a thimble. There was so little liquid that I could hardly taste it. All the wine did was wet my tongue. As I ran my tongue around the thimble getting out the last drop, I didn't know whether I was tasting dandelion wine or silver tarnish. Whatever it was, it wasn't tasty, but then Mama had always claimed that alcoholic beverages looked much better than they tasted.

Uncle Silas downed his wine quickly, and so did Aunt Adelina, but Mama had half of her glass still left when they were finished. She set it down on the tray and went across the room to sit in the smaller chair next to the table.

"Oh, come on now, Cassie," said Uncle Silas. "We may

not be totally defeated. Something could turn up—some new opportunity for me."

"Silas, Silas," burst out Aunt Adelina, "that's just like you, forever looking for pie in the sky and the end of the rainbow." She swung about to face my brother and me, her skirt swishing and the fringes on her polonaise and cuffs swinging. "Silas and Cassie, the children must be told! The fact of the matter is that we are ruined, my dears!"

Ruined? Thunderation, what did that mean? I set my thimble upside down on the tray because it wouldn't stand up otherwise.

Henry Frederick asked, "What does that mean?"

"It means that we have lost all of our money," replied Aunt Adelina.

"Oh," I said, because there didn't seem to be much else for me to say. After that nobody said anything. There was a thick, uncomfortable silence.

Uncle Silas broke the silence after he'd sat down on the gold-velvet settee and rested his hands on his knees. "This past year, 1873, has been a very bad year for business and trade all over the United States. Many men have lost their shirts—lost all of their money, that is. Many men who were at one time happy and rich no longer are happy and rich because they have overextended themselves."

"Overextended?" I asked.

"It means getting too big for your britches," Aunt Adelina explained. "People bought things they couldn't afford to buy. They borrowed money to buy things they planned to sell themselves. They risked too much, and they lost heavily last year."

My brother brightened. "They gambled then, huh?" He knew more than I did about the seamy side of Denton, because he hung around saloons where he said men played cards for money. He never truly went into the back rooms, but he saw the men coming out of them and heard them talking. A couple of times he'd seen Uncle Silas come out of the Payday Saloon. He'd ducked quickly behind some rain barrels so our uncle hadn't seen him. He didn't ever tell anyone but me about this, and I certainly kept his secret.

Our uncle answered, "In a way a lot of men did gamble, I suppose."

"Was it poker or faro, Uncle Silas?" asked Henry Frederick, who although he enjoyed such wickedness was too young to understand that business gambling had nothing at all to do with card games.

"It was not cards, my lad. It was crops and land and farm equipment for the most part."

"Yes." Mama sighed deeply. "Farmers and merchants were the ones who gambled, not saloon loafers."

Our aunt said, "Sit down, both of you, and I'll try to explain what has happened. During this wretched year many farmers borrowed money to buy more farmland and more plows and horses to pull the plows, because they expected to get as good a price for their crops this year as they had been getting for the last few years. With the money from these crops they planned to pay off what they'd borrowed to buy land and equipment. They had gone into debt, you see. Well, to make a long story short, they weren't able to get the good prices. In fact, they got less than half as much for their wheat and other crops this year than they had received just a couple of years ago. Now they can't pay merchants what they owe them for goods bought from their stores, and these merchants who had to borrow money from bankers to stay in business can't pay the banks either."

Though this sounded very grown-up and complicated, I thought I understood it. I put up my hand the way I did at school and said, "Uncle Silas has been selling farm wagons and plows to farmers ever since he sold his sawmill down on the Willamette River, and the farmers hereabouts who bought farm equipment from him can't pay him what they owe him. They owe debts to him. Is that right?"

Aunt Adelina said, "Yes, Lucinda, that is correct. And your uncle is one of the many merchants who has borrowed from the bank. So he owes a debt, too."

I was afraid that I understood again, though I wished I didn't. I put down my hand and with a sinking feeling asked her, "He owes money to Mr. Lambertson's bank?"

"That I do," came from Uncle Silas.

"Indeed Silas does," agreed Aunt Adelina. "This is scarcely a matter to talk to children about at any time, let alone on New Year's Eve, but our owing money to the bank possibly will soon become very important in your lives. You children and your mother may have to go back to Tennessee to your father's family."

I looked at Mama in amazement. To my horror she was nodding. No wonder she'd looked sad all evening. I sat down on the settee next to Uncle Silas and thought about the Howard family back in Tennessee. I didn't remember any of the Howards, although I knew plenty about them from hearsay. There had been four Howard brothers. Three of them had become Johnny Rebs, Confederate soldiers, in the Civil War. But not our papa, who had also been named Henry Frederick. He'd picked the Union side. After he'd been killed, Mama had left Tennessee and gone up to Pennsylvania, where she'd grown up, taking my baby brother and me with her. She'd lived there with her sister, Adelina, and her husband, Silas. Mama knew that the whole Howard family was glad to see her leave Tennessee where we Yankees were an embarrassment to them. If Papa had lived through the War, he would probably have left his home state with us. And more than likely he would have come all the way out to Oregon. Mama said it was something he'd dreamed and talked about before the War began.

Papa's wanting to go West was one of the reasons why we had come out with the Westlakes by ox-drawn covered wagon in 1865, after an old friend of Uncle Silas's had come to Pennsylvania and told them that Oregon was "booming with prosperity." I knew that Mama had written to the oldest Howard brother after the Civil War telling the family we were in the Willamette Valley in Oregon. I knew, too, that she'd never received an answer to her letter.

"What are we going to do in Tennessee?" I asked.

"Heaven only knows, dear," said Mama, "but somebody in the Howard family will surely take us in, though not in eagerness. At least we have enough money to pay for our railroad fares back there."

Knowing that we had some money made me feel better, so I said to my mother, "Then, because we Howards have some money, we aren't ruined. Let's give our money to Uncle Silas right now."

"I can't take money from you folks," he told us. "The way

my luck is going it would be like sending good money after bad. I might lose it, too."

"Well, you children," Aunt Adelina put a sudden end to that sort of talk, "the New Year's celebration is over and it's ten o'clock. Time for you to go up to bed. Kiss your mother good-night and get up there with you. We adults have some talking to do down here in the parlor. We're going to try to think of ways and means to keep from losing this house to the bank."

The house, too? This information astonished me. Thunderation, this big, white-frame house on Poplar Street was the only place I'd ever considered home. I had no memory at all of Tennessee and scarcely any of crossing the country in a covered wagon. It was a nice house, built from boards that Uncle Silas's sawmill had made. It was full of good furniture; most of it had come around Cape Horn by sailing ship and had been bought in Portland by Uncle Silas, who had paid fancy prices. We had one of the most elegant homes in Denton, almost as elegant as the Lambertson house, which I knew very well because my best friend at school was Caralee Lambertson. I looked quickly around our parlor, seeing the marble-top tables, red-and-gold, velvet-upholstered chairs, gold settee, bronze-colored, silk-brocade portieres, and the big, flowery Brussels carpet.

The Westlakes certainly didn't look ruined—even if they were. I was very comfortable here. I had a bedroom all to myself, a four-poster canopy bed, with ruffled, white-muslin hangings, and cherry-wood furniture. The Poplar Street house even had a guest bedroom. We had lots of company, mostly business gentlemen, friends of our uncle. Sometimes there had been so many guests here that Mrs. Apley, who came in three times a week to help, complained about all the extra work and laundry.

Aunt Adelina caught my eyes wandering about the parlor, where the green boughs of Christmas were still pinned up over the red bunting on the mantel. She said, "No, Lucinda, we aren't going to have to move out tomorrow. Now you and your brother please leave us and go up to bed."

My brother got up after I did and lumbered out of the room ahead of me. I let him go on, then asked, "Are we still going to have a roasted goose for New Year's Day dinner or will that be different, too?"

"Yes, there will be a goose. At least there will be this year. I only hope there won't be an unwelcome guest to help us eat it. Now, *please* go to bed."

I left the parlor immediately. Caralee's Christmas-present copy of *The Man in the Iron Mask* was with me, and I planned to read by lamplight till midnight. I was still interested in seeing how the book came out, but not as interested as I had been because of what Aunt Adelina had said. And who might the unwelcome dinner guest be? I wondered.

I walked past the portieres that divided the parlor from the hallway, but instead of going upstairs, I came closer to the draperies and hid behind a long one. Eavesdropping wasn't only a sinful thing, it was downright dangerous. But there might be some more talk about our having to return to Tennessee. That was worrying me, and I knew from the looks on Mama's and Henry Frederick's faces that they were worried, too.

Uncle Silas's deep voice came first. "It's my goose that's cooked, I guess. It's sad that poor child felt she had to ask about her New Year's Day dinner. It isn't as if we are starving."

"Not yet anyhow," Aunt Adelina answered briskly, "but you've had to close down your store, and you've had your desk and office furniture brought here and stored in the carriage house."

I thought he sounded annoyed when he said, "Don't rub it in, Adelina. Soon I hope to carry on my business enterprises somewhere—somehow. I may be done, but I am not licked!"

Her words were sharp. "What do you have in mind this time, Silas Westlake? How I wish you had never sold that sawmill! It was your finest business enterprise."

Mama put in before he could speak up, "Perhaps, Silas, you could make a new start in business with the money I've been saving since we came out to Oregon? I don't want to go back East. I don't even know for certain that the Howards got my letter. I am very doubtful of our welcome there, but I didn't want the children to worry, so I said something else."

Aunt Adelina's words were as harsh as her voice. "Cassie, I have no doubt at all. They won't welcome you. The most they will do is feed and shelter you and make you feel like poor relations. Let's make a promise to each other right now. We won't do anything at all until Silas has spoken with Mr. Bradshaw tomorrow. He's our last hope, but I must admit that I haven't much faith in him, and I really don't look forward to seeing him grin out of his whiskers tomorrow. Oh, Silas, I don't know what ever got into your head to cosign that man's note at the bank."

"I don't know either now, Adelina. It seemed like a good

idea at the moment. Mr. Bradshaw has some very winning ways about him. He's a real go-getter."

"Yes, a go-getter at getting other men's money away from them. Banker Lambertson would never have loaned Barlow Bradshaw any money without your signing the note, too. You let yourself be talked into saying you'd pay off Bradshaw's three-hundred-dollar note if Bradshaw couldn't do it."

I gasped silently at the large amount of money. That was almost a royal ransom. I could figure out what had happened. I knew Mr. Bradshaw, the ginger-whiskered man who used to own the Denton Livery Stable and was now in some sort of horse-and-carriage business up in Portland. Uncle Silas had been mixed up in business with him before, and because of him he owed three hundred dollars to the bank.

No, 1873 hadn't been a good year at all for the Westlakes, and now it seemed it had been a bad one for us Howards, too. We were the Westlakes' permanent guests—had been for years and years. No doubt about it, we were "poor relations," but they had never let us know it, and we loved them for it.

The portiere nearest me smelled dusty. There'd been more rain than usual this year, so Mrs. Apley hadn't taken the portieres and rugs outside to air them yet. I could feel my nose getting stuffed up from the dust. A minute more of eavesdropping, and I might sneeze.

So I turned about and started for the steps. Before I was halfway up them, tiptoeing as quietly as I could, I heard Aunt Adelina say, "My motto for 1874 is going to be 'Onward.' I have no true hope of Mr. Bradshaw paying off his debt, Silas, if you really want to know. I just wish we didn't have to let Mrs. Apley go. Poor Eleanora. What will she do? I am praying that something will happen to keep us all in this house—and out of the poorhouse—and that we shall end the year out of debt. I have taken up the matter with Mr. Whitlow, and from now on I plan to ask his advice on every single move we make, no matter how trifling. I hate to bother him, but I must."

Mr. Whitlow? He gave me the willies. I took a deep breath and went up the rest of the steps as fast as I could. When Aunt Adelina called on *him*, the only place I wanted to be was in bed with the covers pulled up over my head. Mr. Whitlow was her spirit guardian. She said everybody had one—me, too. Well, perhaps I did, but if so, I hadn't made his or her acquaintance yet! Uncle Silas and Mama, who'd been hearing about Mr. Whitlow for years, weren't flustered by him anymore. Henry Frederick and I were, though. Aunt Adelina said he wasn't a ghost, but we weren't convinced.

My brother didn't like it when she'd sometimes say she felt a chilly breeze blowing on her neck and face and would tilt her head to look up at the ceiling. "Is that you come calling, dear Mr. Whitlow?" she would ask. She'd seem to listen for a moment, then smile and nod, and say, "Thank you."

That gave me the willies every time. She'd done that once right in front of company. Mr. Whitlow had come "calling" one wet afternoon last year when Caralee Lambertson had been sitting in our parlor with us, looking at our newest stereopticon slides of Laplanders herding reindeer.

Aunt Adelina had sat tatting lace on the gold settee, talking with us about Lapland, but all at once she had stopped her shuttle, closed her eyes, and asked, "Oh, yes, Mr. Whitlow, I know you're here with us now. May I ask you a question?" She'd waited a moment while Caralee gaped at me, then she'd said, "Shall we buy that little chestnut mare from Mr. Bradshaw?"

I'd turned pink with humiliation while Caralee's brown eyes had darted around the parlor, looking first at the seats, then under the chairs and tables. She'd whispered to me while Aunt Adelina's eyes were still closed, "Who is he? Where is he? I don't see anybody."

I mumbled, "He's a friend of Aunt Adelina's. He gives her messages."

And right afterward had come a small banging sound from the other side of the cottage organ.

"Thank you, Mr. Whitlow, we shall certainly not buy the horse then." And my aunt was back at her tatting.

Caralee put down the stereopticon viewer, leaned over, and whispered again, "Is somebody inside the organ?"

I told her, "I don't know. I've never seen Mr. Whitlow. She says he's a spirit person."

Caralee's eyes had glazed over like amber-colored marbles. I knew what she was thinking, so I'd said, "Aunt Adelina says he's a guardian spirit, and she's as sane as anybody else in this house. She says everybody's got a guardian spirit. Maybe she's right. I used to have a make-believe friend when I was little. Didn't you have one, too?" I was babbling by now. "Well, she's my aunt, and we live with her and she's nice to us, and that's enough for me."

After school, days later, Caralee had asked me, "What does your aunt say that her spirit person looks like?"

"I don't know. I never asked her."

As we walked along in the drizzle, Caralee said, "Lucinda, I talked to my mother about your aunt and her spirit person, and Mama talked to the Reverend Curley. Mr. Curley says he believes your aunt is a spiritualist. He's heard of them. He says they're quite unusual."

This talking about us behind our backs got my goat, so I said, "This is a free country, isn't it? Everyone has a right to believe whatever they want, don't they? If my Aunt Adelina says she's got a guardian spirit, I can't say that she hasn't got one." And then I thought of something to say that should stop everybody from criticizing my aunt's behavior. "Thunderation, Caralee, your mother and Mr. Curley believe in angels, don't they?"

"Of course, they do. Everybody does."

"Well, Aunt Adelina says Mr. Whitlow is an angel, her guardian-spirit angel. Have you ever set eyes on an angel? Has your mother seen one, or the Reverend Curley?"

"I don't know about him, but I know I never have."

"Ha! That settles it then. If *you* can believe in something you can't see, why can't Aunt Adelina?"

Caralee had paused with her brown umbrella behind her beauteous head of long, Scotch-broom-yellow ringlets to say, "Lucinda, it isn't the same, and you know it isn't. Angels don't make cottage organs go bang when somebody asks them a question."

"How do you know what angels would do if you asked them?" I pointed at her. "Go ask Mr. Curley about that."

"No, I won't." She was getting angry, so I knew I was doing well in the argument. "I'm not going to talk to you at all about angels or guardian anythings. Mama says Aunt

Adelina is a very lovely lady, and she wants to keep her as a sewing-circle friend. But Mama doesn't care to hear anything about her old Mr. Whitlow. And if you and I are going to stay friends, neither do I." Her voice changed. "Oh, Lucinda, let's not fight about something nobody but your aunt can see. After all, you and Henry Frederick go to the Reverend Curley's church with us on Sundays. You aren't spiritualists."

"No, we aren't. All right, Caralee, we won't fight about this anymore, but I think I ought to tell Mama how you feel."

That night I caught Mama alone out in the kitchen washing china teacups and told her everything that had been said. Mama sighed as she handed me the last cup to dry. "We are guests in this house, Lucinda. It isn't my place to tell Adelina how to behave in her own home, but I'll try to mention that her spirit friend could make trouble for you with your school friends. I'll suggest as tactfully as I can that she contact her spirits in the presence of only family members."

I caught the word she had used. "*Spirits?* Golly, are there more than just Mr. Whitlow?"

"Oh, yes, Adelina claims she is in touch with an entire Indian tribe and some ancient Egyptians, too. All of them were once alive here on this planet, she says."

I almost dropped the cup I was wiping. "Mr. Whitlow, too?" I asked.

"Well, yes, him, too." Mama spoke reluctantly.

"He was? Oh, Mama, who was he then?"

"Never you mind. It could dismay you if you found out."

I told her, "I'm already dismayed by all those Indians and the Egyptians."

"Lucinda," she said, "we are not going to discuss those spirits anymore, do you hear me?"

After I'd finished drying the dishes, I left the kitchen, feeling both curious and dismayed.

Well, I had thought that I was dismayed then, but I didn't know what the word really meant until that final night of 1873.

I couldn't read half as much of *The Man in the Iron Mask* as I'd hoped to because I couldn't keep my mind on it, and I couldn't fall asleep either. When midnight came, I was wide awake, sitting up in bed. I could hear bells being rung and pistols fired, which was Denton's way of showing in 1874.

Thunderation, but it seemed to me that I'd surely taken on a large load of worry in the course of only a couple of hours.

But all at once I was comforted by something I had just thought of. Aunt Adelina had asked Mr. Whitlow about the chestnut mare that Mr. Bradshaw, who still owned the livery stable at that time, had wanted to sell to Uncle Silas. Mr. Whitlow's advice to her had been not to buy the horse. Well, sir, Mr. Whitlow had been right as could be. Dr. Trumbull had bought her and lived to regret it. That poor horse had become spavined within a month and had to be put out to pasture, so the doctor had to buy a new horse for his carriage.

I hadn't truly expected sunshine the next morning, not in Oregon in January, but it would have made me feel more like facing New Year's Day. Aunt Adelina, dressed in a long white apron, was in the kitchen, getting the goose ready for the oven. She only nodded at me, frowning, then pointed to a pot on the stove. "Your oatmeal is there, Lucinda, and you'll find the cream and sugar where it always is. And as long as you aren't sitting down yet, would you please pour me another cup of coffee?"

"All right." I lifted the big graniteware pot and poured coffee into a cup and brought it to her at the kitchen worktable, where she was struggling with the slippery plucked goose, which was nearly half as big as she was. I wondered if Mr. Whitlow had told her anything after I'd gone up to bed. I would like to know what he said—*after* he said it. But instead I asked, eating my oatmeal, "Isn't Mr. Bradshaw supposed to come here today to see Uncle Silas?"

She answered by saying, "I hope you enjoyed eavesdropping on our conversation last night out in the hall, Lucinda."

"What?" I held my dripping spoon in midair, just below my jaw.

"You revealed yourself by asking about Mr. Bradshaw. We didn't begin to talk about that man until you and your brother had been sent up to bed. I know you were listening because I saw the toes of your boots below the edge of the draperies." She looked hard at me. "Perhaps you wonder why I didn't tell your mother what you were up to. Let it be a lesson to you. People who eavesdrop on other people's private talk deserve to hear bad news. And what did you hear but the wretched tidings that your Uncle Silas not only owes money to the Denton Bank, but he owes Mr. Bradshaw's three hundred dollars to boot?"

"Nothing, and I can truthfully say that I'm sorry I disobeyed." I started in on my oatmeal again. For a moment I thought Mr. Whitlow had somehow told her what I'd done.

"Did you enjoy your wine?"

"No, the thimble tasted like tarnish."

She chuckled. "Next year you'll have half a glass with us, Lucinda. After all, you pick the dandelion blossoms for the wine I make every year. It's such a pretty wine, too."

I asked again, "When will Mr. Bradshaw be arriving?" I was still in my dressing gown with my hair in kid curlers and didn't want to be seen by anybody outside of my family.

"He's supposed to stay at the Denton House Hotel because he's sold his home here and lives in Portland now. He's to come at ten o'clock. I just hope he won't stay on and on until I am forced to ask him to dinner with us."

The hallway clock had just bonged out eight, so I had plenty of time. I finished my oatmeal, put the dish under the kitchen pump, and filled it with water to soak. Then, before I went upstairs with a cup of coffee for Mama, who was sleeping in, I started to ask my aunt about Mr. Bradshaw's new line of business in Portland.

I had the words ready in my mind when all at once there came a scratching at the kitchen door. The door had a piece of clear glass set in the top panel, and I looked at it to see who was there. *There was no face to be seen!* Thunderation! My hair stood straight up on the back of my neck. Mr. Whitlow? Outside this time?

But then there was a knock, and right afterward came a thin, little voice, "Missus Westlake, it's me, lemme in. I got a letter for you."

I let out a sigh of relief and told my knees to stop shaking. It was only Zenobia Apley, who was eight years old and not tall enough yet to reach the glass in the top of the door. She was the younger of Mrs. Apley's two girls. I went to the door, opened it, and there she was bundled up to the eyes in a muffler and yellow oilskin coat, which was so big on her that it came all the way down to her rubber boots. She had on her mother's sou'wester hat. Tilting her head way back so that I could see her reddish-yellow braids and her slanting, greenish eyes, she said, "Lucinda, is your Uncle Silas here? A man at the Denton House Hotel paid me a nickel when I was passing by to fetch this here letter to him before he got on the stagecoach."

My aunt was at the door at once, wiping her hands on the apron. "I'll take that letter, Zenobia."

"Wait till I find it, Missus Westlake."

Sniffing, Zenobia reached one hand deep down to the side of the raincoat and hauled out a brown envelope. She told Aunt Adelina, "There's some words from him I'm supposed to say, too. Lemme think about what they are."

"What are they, dear?" asked my aunt, as she took the letter, which had gone limp with rainwater.

Zenobia's pale, squinting eyes were fixed on the ceiling, and her voice was hoarse while she recited, "The man said for me to tell Mr. Westlake that what's inside this here envelope is the best he can do right now. He says to tell you it's all he's got to spare."

My aunt asked with a frown on her face, "Zenobia, think very hard. Is that *all* you were to tell Silas?"

The little girl was also frowning. Suddenly she shook her head and came out with, "Nope." Her lips moved without sound for a moment; then she said, "He said for me to tell

Mr. Westlake the best of luck and good-bye and that he's off to California. Then he handed me the letter and the nickel and told me to skedaddle over here. And I skedaddled!"

Aunt Adelina's teeth were almost clenched when she said, "It seems that Mr. Barlow Bradshaw won't be coming here today after all." She snorted, then spoke to the Apley girl. "Thank you, Zenobia. Take a cookie from the cookie jar." She turned to me. "Lucinda, please go upstairs and tell your uncle that Mr. Bradshaw has skipped out on him. Ask him to come down and get the letter, please. It's his letter. I won't open it!"

"Yes, ma'am." Forgetting my mother's coffee, I left for the front stairs at the same moment Zenobia left through the kitchen door, with a sugar cookie in each hand.

CHAPTER II

The Brown Envelope

I rapped on the door of the master bedroom, and while I waited for Uncle Silas to answer it, I bit at a hangnail. Alas, I'd understood what Zenobia had said, and I understood what Aunt Adelina had meant. Mr. Bradshaw had skedaddled. He'd skipped Oregon entirely. That development looked bad.

But I had some hope that the Westlakes weren't ruined absolutely. There was still that long, brown envelope Bradshaw had given Zenobia. And there had been a message that all he could spare was in it. That must mean some money was inside. I surely hoped so for Uncle Silas's sake. Maybe the envelope contained almost the full three hundred dollars.

He came to the door in his long brown-velvet dressing

35

gown and carpet slippers. Uncle Silas didn't look too chipper. He probably hadn't slept well last night. I gave him the message, and he scowled down at me. "Bradshaw left town, huh? Well, I can't say that I am very surprised. But you did say, didn't you, that he sent a letter by little Yolanda Apley to me?"

"It was Zenobia, the younger sister, who brought it, Uncle Silas."

"No matter. I can't tell those two kids apart. I don't know how their mother does either. All right, Lucinda, I'll be right down."

I'd finished my breakfast, but I didn't go to my bedroom to get dressed. No, I went back to the kitchen just ahead of Uncle Silas, because I wanted to know what was in that envelope, too.

The goose was in the oven now. There was only one thing on the table: the brown envelope.

I saw the big, black-ink handwriting on it. It said, *For: Silas Theophilus Westlake, Esquire.*

I told my aunt, "He's coming right down." Then I sat in a chair at the kitchen table opposite her.

She didn't say anything but only nodded at me.

I could hear Uncle Silas huffing and puffing down the stairs and along the hall before I could see him. It didn't seem to me that he was in any great hurry to find out what was in Mr. Bradshaw's letter.

"There it is, Silas," were Aunt Adelina's first words, as she pointed to the table.

He picked up the letter and, with his blond eyebrows gathered together in a frown, opened it. First, he took out some greenbacks, fluttered them through his fingers, and said, "Only forty-eight dollars, Adelina."

She asked quietly, "Is that *all* there is in the envelope, Silas?"

"That's all the money there is."

"You have been cogged, Silas."

I knew that slang word. It meant the same as hoodwinked or hornswoggled or cheated.

"Isn't there *anything* else in it?" I couldn't help asking, even if it wasn't any of my business.

"Yes, there's this piece of paper, whatever it is." He drew out a sheet of paper, unfolded it, and read down it. Then he laughed sharply and flung it down. "Bradshaw writes here that an old Indian medicine man gave this to him a long time ago. It's the recipe for a medicine called the Tuscarora Tonic."

"What would that be worth, Uncle Silas?"

"It appears to me that it's not worth a red cent, Lucinda. It seems to be just some weeds from the wilderness. Here you look at it yourself. Bradshaw didn't even write down what particular sickness it's supposed to cure. All sickness under the sun, more than likely."

I arose, got the paper, and brought it over to the table. The handwriting didn't match that on the envelope, so it wasn't anything Bradshaw had written. It was thin writing, like spider webs. I read off some of the things in it but not their amounts. "Aunt Adelina, it says, 'ginger, cinnamon, sage, saffron, and cloves.' It sounds like a cake recipe. No, I take that back. There's lots more here, too." Now I read more slowly because I'd never heard of these things before, "'spikenard root, angelica root, comfrey, tansy, mugwort, pennyroyal, rue, valerian, sneezewort, Saint-John's-wort and hog's fennel,' and some other things I won't try to twist my tongue around."

"Lucinda, what's the solvent?" asked my aunt.

"The what?"

"What makes up the liquid part of the tonic?"

"Oh, that." I looked at the very bottom of the long, long list of things on the paper and read, "It says to 'boil in spirits, strain, bottle, and seal.' What are spirits?"

"In this case spirits means alcohol in some form—wine or whiskey or something of that sort."

"Oh." I thought now of the bottles of medicine I'd seen on one shelf of Mr. Quincy's General Store. They were big bottles, full to the cork with dark liquids. I'd read some of the labels. Some of the medicines were supposed to cure everything from gumboils, crooked spines, and housemaid's knee to being struck down by lightning.

Aunt Adelina reached out to me. "Please let me see that miserable Bradshaw's formula, Lucinda."

I handed it over to my aunt, who put it down on the kitchen table and ran her hand over it, smoothing the paper out. She read it slowly and carefully, while Uncle Silas got himself a cup of coffee. After she finished, she said, "It's been a long time since I did this sort of thing, but I think I can still make out some parts of it. Yes, it seems to be a tonic all right. Some of the herbs and roots are blood purifiers and strengtheners of the whole body. Some others help headache and stop hysteria, and then, of course, Saint-John's-wort is for overcoming a heavy feeling of sadness."

Uncle Silas told her, "That's what I need, Adelina—a peck of Saint-John's-wort right now."

"Yes, of course, Silas." She wasn't paying too much attention to him until she said all at once, "Silas, when you go down to the bank tomorrow to ask for more time to pay back the money you owe, I want to go with you. I want to see Banker Lambertson, too."

"Adelina, I forbid it. It isn't a woman's place. No bank is. You stay here. I got us into this trouble, and I'll get us out of it. You'd only come on full chisel and make Lambertson so angry that he'd tell me, 'No, I won't give you more time,' even faster."

I said, "Caralee Lambertson is my best friend in the whole wide world, Uncle Silas."

He shook his head. "That won't matter with her father, Lucinda. Money means more to most bankers than anybody's friendship, including his own best friends. Lamberston has told a lot of desperate men no in his time."

"How many women has he said no to?" asked my aunt.

"Not as many because not as many ladies ask to borrow money. But I'm pretty sure that Lambertson would turn down a lady just as fast as a man if she didn't have good security to put up."

"What's that?" I knew what *security* was but not the way my uncle was using the word.

He didn't explain. "It isn't anything I want to talk about right at this moment, Lucinda."

Aunt Adelina sighed. Then she did the explaining, and I understood why Uncle Silas didn't want to. "Child, this house is security. So is your uncle's business. Your uncle had to promise to sell both the house and business to get the money to pay off the bank if he couldn't pay that debt any other way. He had to use this house and his business to back up the loan from the bank. It's to make the bank feel secure, you see."

Again, I thought I understood, even if I didn't like to. I asked, "Won't the bank take Mr. Bradshaw's forty-eight dollars?"

"Of course, it will, but that is only a drop in the bucket of what we owe."

Uncle Silas stared out the kitchen window at the rain.

I almost wailed. "But what are we going to do? We Howards don't want to go back to Tennessee where we'll be treated like poor relations. Nobody really wants Mama and Henry Frederick and me back there. We want to stay here with our relatives we love."

One of my aunt's bony little hands came over the tabletop to gather up one of mine. To my surprise her hand felt as strong as horseshoe iron. I didn't know there was so much strength in her tiny body. She said, "You aren't going back there. We all are going to stay right here in Denton. We'll tighten our belts and try to hang on here. They'll have to come and carry out the furniture before I'll leave this house. And they're going to have to carry *me* out because I'll be on the settee."

"Adelina!" Uncle Silas turned away from the window to look at his wife in a scandalized way.

She got up and told him, "Silas, if Mr. Lambertson doesn't give you more time on your loan, we're going to have a council of war tomorrow afternoon. I take it that you don't mind giving this formula for the Tuscarora Tonic to me, do you?"

He came out with that sharp, unhappy laugh again. "Why should I? I can afford to do that at least." There was an ink bottle and a steel-tip pen on the table next to the pepper shaker. He opened the bottle, dipped the pen, and while I looked on wrote on one side of Bradshaw's paper. "I give this recipe to my beloved wife, Adelina Westlake, January 1, 1874," and he signed it with his full name.

Then he laughed and handed it to Aunt Adelina, who folded and put it into her deep apron pocket. "Thank you, Silas," she told him.

Slowly I went upstairs to get dressed. I was unhappy, too, unhappy for the Westlakes and for us Howards and for Mrs. Apley, who didn't know yet that she was going to have to look for work somewhere else. Mrs. Apley had come over to clean or help serve at parties ever since the Westlake house had been built five years ago.

Mrs. Apley was a widow like Mama, but her husband hadn't been killed in the Civil War. Mr. Apley had been cutting down trees in a lumber camp and been killed by a falling tree. He had been sawing it in two when he stopped to light his pipe and without thinking leaned on the tree. The accident had happened up in Washington Territory where some of the Apleys lived. Afterward Mrs. Apley had lived up north for a while, then over in Idaho Territory, and finally had come down to Denton because that's where her elderly mother lived. When her mother had died, Mrs. Apley, who was poor, had gone to work cleaning people's houses. According to Aunt Adelina, that was the only work most ladies knew anything about, which was a very great pity. Yolanda had been just a tot when the Apleys came to Denton and Zenobia only a baby in arms. Sometimes I'd looked after the two little girls out on the front veranda or in the kitchen when Mrs. Apley came to work for my aunt. When I was at school, Mrs. Apley left them with a neighbor of hers.

I combed out my braids and put blue ribbons on the ends; then I got into my petticoats, gown, and pinafore. All the while I went on thinking about the terrible troubles we were having. It didn't seem fair that Mrs. Apley was going to have to suffer because Uncle Silas was ruined. It was different with us Howards because we were permanent guests of the Westlakes and should by rights be ruined, too.

From thinking about the Apleys, my mind went to Aunt Adelina. My, but she had seemed to know quite a bit about plants—"weeds from the wilderness," as Uncle Silas had jokingly called them. I wondered where she'd learned what they were used for. There weren't any books in the house that told things like that, though there were recipe books for things like apple grunt and sea-clam jam.

And why had she asked Uncle Silas to give her the tonic recipe? Thunderation! Did she plan to make some of that stuff? Where would she get all of those queer things a person needed to make it the way the Tuscarora Indians did?

And then there was the matter of the solvent. Aunt Adelina made dandelion wine every year, and sometimes Uncle Silas brought a bottle of port wine into the house, but she didn't hold with whiskey or rum or other strong drinks. I'd never heard the word *spirits* used before except when she talked to the family about Mr. Whitlow.

Well, I would have to do some more thinking on this. Now

I'd have something more important to consider than how my waistline was going to turn out when I was grown-up. It was an enormous twenty-one inches now. My hope was to have it down to a proper sixteen inches by the time I was twenty years old. That was what most American ladies' waists were at that age, except for Aunt Adelina, who refused to wear corsets at all. Getting my waist down to sixteen inches would mean starting to wear corsets when I was fourteen and from then on suffering in silence for the sake of beauty. Caralee and I planned to suffer together and measure each other's waists the first Saturday of each month. Sometimes we'd probably have to starve, the way most ladies did. We'd do that together, too, we'd decided.

But I hadn't got laced into my first corset yet, so I could still eat. I looked forward to this New Year's Day dinner and was I ever glad Mr. Bradshaw, the skipper-outer, wasn't going to be with us. Pretty soon I'd be able to smell the roast goose in the oven. We weren't going to take in our belts today; we'd do that later. I supposed we wouldn't be having geese and beef joints so often anymore. Oh well, eating less tasty things could take a girl's appetite away and help her whittle down her waist.

I nodded at my face in the mirror as I fiddled with the bows at the end of my pigtails. I wished my hair was golden yellow like Caralee Lambertson's, and, at the same time, I wished Uncle Silas had the gold that her papa had in his bank.

And then I got an idea, which I thought would be a very good one once I got started on it!

Naturally, Henry Frederick and I had to go back to school

on January 2. I managed to finish reading *The Man in the Iron Mask* on New Year's Day, so I was ready to return Caralee's copy of it to her. I planned to give it back to her at recess.

Miss Hinkle, our teacher, always made her pupils go outside to get some fresh air—or so she said—even when it was raining. I privately thought she was saving herself from having to look at us for those fifteen, refreshing minutes. Caralee and I stood together outside the schoolroom in our oilskins, under a tall, dripping evergreen, talking about the book, which had been very thrilling, although not as thrilling to me as *The Three Musketeers*.

After discussing the books, I got down to brass tacks. I'd been waiting all morning to have this time alone with Caralee, and I wanted to make the most of it. I'd even asked my brother to keep the other kids away from us so I wouldn't be interrupted. He'd pulled off a boy's cap, and everyone was chasing him around the schoolhouse's muddy grounds while he shouted and waved the stolen cap in the air.

I came straight to the point. "Caralee, Mr. Barlow Bradshaw has run away down to California and left Uncle Silas to pay off the three hundred dollars Bradshaw owes your father. What do you think of that?"

She almost snapped at me. "Lucinda, it isn't my father's money. It isn't my father your uncle is supposed to pay back. It's the Bank of Denton."

"But your father *is* the bank, Caralee."

This time she did snap. "He only works there. He's the most important person there, but he doesn't *own* the bank."

I said, "Uncle Silas is going to go down today and ask

your father to give him some more time to pay what he owes him."

Caralee rubbed the end of her nose with her red mitten, frowned, and said without snapping at me this time, "Oh, Lucinda, I wish this wasn't happening. I wish there weren't such hard times in the country. Papa says last year is going to go down in history books as a bad year. I wish all those men hadn't borrowed all that money. It's all Papa talks about these days. It makes him feel unhappy, too."

"It's all my aunt and uncle talk about now. They're sure worried."

She nodded. "Everybody is. Papa told me that it isn't good for banks in hard times either."

I couldn't see how that could be. Mr. Lambertson had loaned out money, so that meant to me that he had money to lend. Uncle Silas certainly didn't—not anymore.

Caralee went on, "Lucinda, I don't think Papa will give your uncle more time to pay what he owes the bank. Papa says lots of men here in Denton and farmers out in the Willamette Valley, too, are coming to him asking for more time to pay their debts to the bank. He tells almost all of them no. He says he has to say that."

I let out a low wail that made her look at me in a startled way. I said, "Then we can't be best friends anymore," I said. "We're ruined. We have to let Mrs. Apley go and take in our belts and eat less, I guess."

"Lucinda!" She fell on my neck. "Oh, Lucinda!"

"Oh, Caralee!" I fell on her neck. "There's worse than that. Mama and Henry Frederick and I might have to go back to Tennessee where the Howards come from. That's thousands of miles away. They were Confederates during the Civil War. They'll hold us prisoner back there, so we'll never see each other again."

She cried out, "Tennessee? All the way back there! I'll tell Papa what you said. He won't want you to go away. Neither will Mama because she likes your mother. Will your aunt and uncle go away, too?"

"I don't think they plan to. Aunt Adelina says we'll stay here, no matter what, but I don't know how we can, Caralee."

She nodded. "I'll tell Papa that the Westlakes aren't going to skip out the way Mr. Bradshaw did. That ought to make him think better of your Uncle Silas." Her voice sank to a whisper. "Has your aunt asked her spirit, that Mr. Whitlow, about this yet?"

"I don't know, but I think she plans to. Do you want me to tell you what he says to her?"

Caralee shivered along with me as she said, "In a way I do, and in a way I don't. I've tried over and over to forget about that scarey rapping from the organ, but I heard it. And he was certainly right about the chestnut mare with the spavins."

All I could say was, "I haven't heard the cottage organ banging lately when nobody was playing it, Caralee."

"Lucinda, I'll do whatever I can to help you out. First of all, I'll talk to Papa, but I don't think it will do any good. Haven't any of you Howards got any money?"

"I don't. Henry Frederick doesn't, and all Mama has is enough to get us back to Tennessee on the train."

*   *   *

Caralee was as right as the rain that kept falling all that day.

Her father did tell Uncle Silas no. Nobody was really surprised because I'd warned them before Uncle Silas came home late that afternoon.

He looked quite a bit the worse for wear as he came inside. His first words were, "He wouldn't give me any more time, Adelina." From the bank he'd gone to the Payday Saloon with some other men who'd also been told no by Banker Lambertson. All of them had been downcast, too. When he'd heard their bad news, Mr. Gustave Heffer, who owned the Payday, had given these men whatever they wanted to drink and not charged them for it.

"That was nice of Mr. Heffer. Why did he do that?" asked Aunt Adelina in a voice that wasn't as sharp as it used to be when she spoke of the short, skinny saloonkeeper.

"Because at heart he's a generous soul, Adelina. He understands what it's like to be turned down by someone. He told us all about it this afternoon. I saw a tear roll down his cheek into his beer."

"Who did that to him? Banker Lambertson?" I wanted to know. "Who turned down Mr. Heffer?" It seemed to me that the Payday Saloon's owner was a prosperous man. He surely was an elegant dresser. He had one of the biggest whiskey saloons in Denton, and he had it repainted bright yellow every other year to keep it looking nicer than the other fourteen saloons.

After he'd got his oilskins off, Uncle Silas said, "No, it wasn't the banker in his case. It was a lady. It takes a woman to reduce a strong man to tears."

"Pshaw!" hooted Aunt Adelina, while Mama smiled at this silly notion. "Well, Silas, out with it. Tell us Heffer's tale of woe. It could gladden our ears to hear that someone else in this country is down at heart because of something other than debts and business failures." She picked up her tatting shuttle and started her fingers flying, turning out lace to trim the hems of pillow cases. Clearly she expected this to be a long and interesting story.

Mama did, too. She started to crochet. Taking a hint from them, I put down the stereopticon viewer and stared expectantly at my uncle.

"Oh, sit down, Silas," came from my aunt. "We are all ears."

"Adelina, I can see that! You know this is really Gus Heffer's business, and not anybody else's."

"Nonsense," said Aunt Adelina, "if Heffer told you and a group of other men in a public place, which is exactly what a saloon is, he can't expect to be hugging a deep, dark secret to his bosom."

Uncle Silas remained on his feet. "That's why he's sad. He won't be hugging to his bosom the beautiful lady he had in mind to marry."

"Did she die?" I asked quickly. How interesting. It seemed to me that a lot of beautiful ladies—especially in the books Caralee and I had read in the last year or two—had died before their time.

"No, Lucinda, not that. The lady returned all of the money Heffer had sent her to come out to Oregon on the railroad."

Aunt Adelina said, with acid in her tone, "At least he can say he got *his* money back!"

"Yes, but the pretty little widow in Kansas City didn't come. He's been trying to marry her for thirty years, but it somehow never works out."

"Never works out? Thirty years?" asked Mama.

"That's what Gus says. The widow was his childhood sweetheart, but she married another man. When that husband died, she married another one before Gus found out the first one had died. After that, he kept in touch with her by Christmas card. Well, sir, this last time she was left a widow she wrote to Gus, and they had a lively correspondence back and forth for a while. He sent her the money to come out here to Denton to look him over after all these years. He thought he'd propose to her, then, if he still liked her, he—"

Mama interrupted. "He should have gone back to Kansas City instead of asking her to come out here alone." She shook her head.

Uncle Silas went on. "He heard from the widow just today by letter that she was marrying husband number three, a partner of husband number two."

"How long did Mr. Heffer court the widow by mail?" asked Aunt Adelina with a glance at Mama.

"Three years, he says."

"He was far too slow in the matter. Cassie is right. He should have gone back there at the end of the first year."

"Gus knows that now, Adelina," said Uncle Silas. "But at the moment he's a powerfully lonesome man, ladies. Adelina, what would you say if I invited him over for supper some night this week?"

"Silas, if he or anyone else expects a fine supper at this house, he'll have to bring it along with him from now on.

We are going to eat whatever I can get to grow in our garden, along with dried lentils, peas, bread, and, of course, pork. I intend to keep more pigs from now on. A pig is a very good investment."

I groaned inwardly. I didn't like having even the one porker we always kept out behind the carriage house. It was Henry Frederick's chore to feed it, not mine, so I couldn't complain about that. But pigs weren't elegant animals like horses. Caralee agreed with me on that. And now we were going to have more pigs. Grunting, snuffling porkers!

Uncle Silas said, "Mr. Heffer is a nice little gent, Adelina. He means well. He should have married and settled down a long time ago. He'd appreciate a comfortable home and a loving little wife. He'd be danged good to the lucky woman who gets him. Did you hear me, Cassie Howard?"

"*Silas Westlake!*" The name exploded out of Aunt Adelina. "You can't be thinking that Cassandra, my sister, should seriously consider being courted by Mr. Heffer, a saloon-keeper?"

"No, he's shorter than Mama is," I put in swiftly. I didn't think I'd like Mr. Heffer as a stepfather.

Mama said very calmly, "Oh, I don't think that I'm interested in Mr. Heffer."

Feeling better, I said, "He hasn't got very much hair left on his head, although he tries to comb it so it looks like more."

"Yes, sir, that's true about poor little Gus." Uncle Silas ran his hands through his hair, which wasn't quite as thick as it used to be. "Not having a good crop of hair has a deep impact on a man's feelings."

"I am aware of that, Silas," said my aunt, "and I must say that I'm glad it came up naturally in our conversation right now. I've been thinking quite a lot today and yesterday about the hair on a man's head."

"Whatever for, Adelina?" asked Mama.

"I think you're all about to find out why, Cassie. Mr. Whitlow agrees with me. I asked him last night."

I grabbed hold of the back of a chair in my excitement as she turned to Uncle Silas. "I think, don't you, Silas, that it's time for us to take stock of our money situation?"

I let out my breath in disappointment. No, it didn't seem that she was going to talk about Mr. Whitlow. But because I wanted to know about our money troubles and what it had to do with men's baldness, I decided to try and stay.

"May I please hear what you have to say, Uncle Silas?" I asked. "Remember, I'm thirteen now, and I drink wine, and I asked Caralee Lambertson at school today if she'd talk to her father about giving you some more time on your debts. I'm trying to help out."

He nodded. "All right, it appears to me inasmuch as Adelina has told you we are ruined and you saw the envelope from Mr. Bradshaw and have tried to influence the banker's family that you should be present when we tally up our assets."

"What are assets, Uncle Silas?"

"What we own."

"Oh." I thought for a moment. All I owned were some books, a gold locket, and a seed-pearl, coral-studded bracelet.

Mama said, "We Howards have nothing really except for the railroad fare back to the East Coast and some gold coins you've given me over the years as Christmas presents." She let out a very deep sigh. "I've given you all very little, alas."

Aunt Adelina told her, "Nonsense, Cassie, you've given us your company and that of your two fine healthy children in place of those Silas and I never had. You've helped out with the work here when I've entertained. Life wouldn't have been half so pleasant in Oregon without our beloved Howard family. Silas and I have liked protecting you and the children."

"Oh, Silas, oh, Adelina!" Mama stood up, dropping her crocheting, and with her handkerchief to her eyes went out of the room.

I stayed. It was more interesting down here in the parlor than upstairs.

Uncle Silas said, "There's a mortgage on the house, but the payment to the bank isn't due for nearly a year. The debt I owe at the bank isn't due for three months, and the Bradshaw debt doesn't come due for two months. I have a little cash on hand, Adelina. About a hundred dollars in all. I'll try to sell the wagons and buggies I have, but I don't think there'll be many buyers for such things these days."

My aunt nodded her head. "No, more than likely there won't be. Well, Silas, you know the jewelry I have because you gave it all to me over the years. I've never cared much for jewelry, you know. The only item of any real value is the gold lapel watch with the diamonds set on the case. You may have it."

"No, that watch wouldn't fetch you more than fifty dollars, Adelina."

"Fifty dollars is more than nothing. Silas, would you consider giving me Mr. Bradshaw's forty-eight dollars along with the formula for the tonic that you already signed over?"

"What do you plan to do?" I thought my uncle was looking both startled and suspicious.

"Silas, I plan to buy ingredients for the Hopi Hair Restorer and Magnolia Milk Face Powder. I have begun to save eggshells already. Silas, I want to go into business."

There was a long, long silence, while we three listened to the rain dripping softly down the eaves of the veranda roof.

I burst into the quiet with, "What will Mr. Whitlow have to say about that, Aunt Adelina?"

She opened her mouth to say something, but before she could get a word out there was a very loud bang—from the top of the cottage organ this time.

Thunderation! *Mr. Whitlow!* This time he had spoken before a question had even been asked.

CHAPTER III

"This Lady Does, Though!"

Just as if he hadn't heard the bang at all, Uncle Silas objected. "Ladies do not go into business here in Denton, Adelina."

"This lady does, though. I've made eggshell powder to take the redness out of my face for years, though not a soul knows it but Cassie. I have powdered since 1855. And the recipe for hair restorer has been in our family for donkey's years back home in Pennsylvania."

I said, "But what have the Hopi Indians got to do with your hair restorer from back East?"

She said sharply, "Just about as much as the Tuscarora Indians have to do with Mr. Bradshaw's tonic. No Tuscarora ever drank an ounce of it."

55

I asked, "Well, if that's so, why use Indian names?"

"Lucinda, have you ever heard of a bald Indian or a sick one?"

I thought deeply. There were Indians here in **Oregon,** and I had never heard of one who didn't have a full head of hair. Maybe the sick Indians didn't go out much in public, but it was true enough that most of the Indians I'd ever set eyes on were strong looking.

Uncle Silas interrupted my thoughts by saying, "I forbid you, Adelina, to start making things for sale. It would embarrass me."

"Silas Westlake, you are *not* the master of the kitchen, which is where I plan to make my preparations. What I do will have no connection with you. Your name will not be on the products. I'll call myself Mrs. Eastlake, if you'd like."

"But everyone in Denton will know, no matter what you do!"

"Thank heaven, Denton, Oregon, is not the entire country." My aunt's voice deepened, and she spoke more slowly. "Silas, I am asking you for your blessing in my business enterprises."

"You won't be getting it, Adelina. Don't expect it from me. It's not womanly—not ladylike."

"Then at least promise me that you won't try to put obstacles in my path. I want to do this." She looked very solemn now and more than a little bit sad. "I want to prove that I can be in business."

"All right, all right, Adelina. You go ahead and do it. Make me look foolish. I'm going out again now. And I don't want any supper."

She got up. "Where, may I ask, are you going?"

"To the Payday Saloon to tell Gus Heffer that he's a luckier man than he realizes not to be marrying that Kansas City widow."

"That was a low blow, Silas, and unfairly aimed," were Aunt Adelina's last words to him as he went out.

After he'd gone, slamming the front door behind him, there was a silence.

Then Aunt Adelina said to me, "Lucinda, let that be a lesson to you." I didn't quite know what she meant, so I decided that she was speaking about Uncle Silas's stubbornness. After all, she was trying to help him out in his time of trouble.

I said, "I think what you're doing is perfectly splendid. I'll help you if you'll show me how. I'll bet Caralee would help, too. Is it fun to make face powder?"

"It takes muscle, child. Yes, I had expected to ask you and your brother to help me. And perhaps even Caralee." She laughed, but I could tell she was plenty vexed with Uncle Silas. "I doubt, though, if Banker Lambertson will permit his daughter to go house to house here in Denton, taking orders and delivering powder and hair restorer."

"House to house?" I hadn't expected this kind of work. I got up from my chair to stare at her. Making cosmetics in the kitchen might be interesting, but asking people you knew to buy something you'd made didn't sound good at all. It was one thing to collect pennies for the church to send to missionaries in Africa; selling hair grower to your friends' fathers wasn't the same at all.

My aunt must have understood the expression on my face

because she said, "Well, you could very easily have to sell things house to house back in Tennessee, you know. You probably wouldn't be able to go to secondary school there at all because you'd be out working all day."

"That surely isn't very ladylike—working!"

"Are you saying that working for somebody else is not lady-like? You seem to feel it's all right for me to work in my own kitchen where I'm the boss. Lucinda, what is not ladylike is not paying your debts. Why shouldn't a lady work?"

"It's selling things I'm talking about. That's men's work."

"Women work as clerks in dry-goods stores, don't they? And it most certainly is woman's work when a woman can help her family out in an emergency. This is an emergency for both the Westlakes and the Howards, don't you think?"

I didn't look at her but at the cottage organ, expecting to hear another bang from it. None came. I didn't hear anything but the ticktock of the grandfather clock in the hall-way and the plunking sound of the rain on the front-porch floor.

I took a deep breath and told her, "I'll help out. I promise. All you have to do is to ask me."

"I *am* asking you, Lucinda. All you need to do is go door to door here in Denton, smile, give out a leaflet, and then if you're asked about my products, tell the customer what you think he or she needs to know. It will be very simple."

"All right, Aunt Adelina."

I went out of the parlor and up the steps, thinking of all of the men I knew who were completely bald-headed and of those who were almost bald, like Banker Lambertson.

Upstairs I stopped first at Mama's bedroom. "Mama, I need

to talk with you about the Westlakes. You didn't hear what else they said because you'd left already." Then I told her, trying to use the same words my aunt and uncle had used. "Aunt Adelina's bound and determined to go into business, and she wants us to help her," I finished. "Uncle Silas says he won't, and he went off to the Payday Saloon without his supper."

"Oh, my."

"Mama, you've known him for a long time. Has he ever done that before?"

"Not since I've been living with them. The two of them have had some ups and downs and differences of opinion, but Silas has never stormed out like that. He's feeling quite touchy about things at the moment—and no wonder. It is very difficult to be ruined. I think this is the worst business reverse he has ever had."

I asked, "Has he been ruined before?"

"Oh, Lucinda, Adelina told me once that he has been in a great many businesses. Some have gone boom, and some have gone bust."

I was interested in this information. All I had ever heard was that he had sold whale oil back East, and I'd known that he'd been in the stagecoach business here in Oregon and then owned the sawmill. After selling it, Uncle Silas took all the money and went into the farm-equipment business, selling wagons and plows and things like that.

"Why, he sold ladies' boots and slippers and hoops for hoop skirts as a young man and after that sold farms and town lots. During the Civil War he was a sutler. He had a horse and wagon and followed the Union Army, selling tobacco and books and harmonicas and whatever else the soldiers would buy. Your aunt has hinted that he has been in other lines of work, too, as well as forever lending money that isn't paid back to him. He has a soft heart toward his friends."

I had to agree that my uncle had done quite a number of things and some of them not so wise, such as lending money. I wouldn't ever lend money! "He sure doesn't want Aunt Adelina to make those things she says she's going to make," I said.

Mama nodded. "Adelina talked to me about that before she brought it up to him. She had a feeling that he'd have strong objections. Your aunt is a forceful woman when she makes up her mind to be. When we were girls together, she told me that she would like to try to make her mark in the world. Our father would have none of that, believe me! How he used to lecture her. He insisted that there were only two proper ways of life for ladies. The best life of all was that of a respectable married woman. The next best was that of a respectable unwed schoolteacher. He was very pleased when Adelina married your Uncle Silas after a long courtship. He thought she would never get around to marrying."

"Didn't she want to marry him?"

"Let us say that she wasn't eager to marry anyone. She liked working in our father's office, acting as his secretary, replying to the letters he received from all over the East Coast, ordering dried herbs for his shop."

I nodded. I'd known that my grandfather, whom I'd never seen because he had died when I was only a baby, had been a pharmacist, or apothecary. I thought that apothecary and druggist shops were fascinating, with all the strange-smelling things stored in them. I loved all the big and little china jars and the enormous glass bottles filled with red- or green- or blue-colored liquid. I supposed they were tonics for rich, sick people. They must taste wonderful since they were so pretty.

Mama kept on talking. "Lucinda, I never told you this before, but your great grandmother, our father's mother, knew a great deal about herbs and grasses that were used in medicines. She used to gather them in the forests and woods. Adelina went out with her when she was younger than you are. She claims that she remembers what she learned from her and from our father, too."

Ah! This explained why she'd known about the things that went into the Tuscarora Tonic. I said, "Aunt Adelina's fifteen years older than you are. Was your grandma, my great grandmother, alive at the time of the American Revolution?"

"Yes, she said she was, but she was just an infant then."

I counted backward for a time, then said, "Thunderation, that was almost a hundred years ago, wasn't it? Well, Aunt Adelina's out in Oregon now, and the plants that grow here aren't the same ones, are they?"

"No, but she says some are much like their counterparts back East, and she can use substitutes for others."

I thought of dandelions. According to Uncle Silas, Aunt Adelina had always made that wine wherever they'd lived. So I told Mama, "Yes, she means dandelions."

"More than that, Lucinda. She says the Chinook Indians on this coast know the useful native plants."

I let out a sigh. I'd heard about the Tuscarora Indians

today and then the Hopi Indians and now the Chinook Indians. "Thank you for telling me about Uncle Silas. I'll start making up a list of Denton men who are losing their hair or have lost it. When I'm finished with that list, I'll make another of ladies with red noses who might be interested in buying Magnolia Milk Face Powder." Near the door, I turned around to say, "Oh, Mr. Whitlow seems to think Aunt Adelina is doing the right thing. I just now heard him go pop in the cottage organ."

"That will surely give Adelina the courage to go ahead. After all, he was very right about that horse. Your aunt claims spirits know all about the future, and that's surely more than any of us do here in Denton."

"What do you think about Mr. Whitlow now, Mama?" I wondered if she'd done some more pondering about him since I'd asked her to talk to my aunt about being tactful.

"Well, I haven't quite made up my mind whether to be scared out of my wits by him or whether I should start asking him questions myself. If he tells Adelina the right things to do, he must be a very well-intentioned spirit in spite of his past life, which I shall still not discuss with you yet. In any event, he must like your aunt. It seems that he chose to come to her on his own."

I said, "Mama, that business about the chestnut horse wasn't as important as what's happening to us right now. Aunt Adelina tried to get Uncle Silas to give her that forty-eight dollars of Mr. Bradshaw's."

"I knew she had planned to ask him for it. I've already given her part of the cash we had for our fares back to Tennessee."

With my hand on the doorknob, I asked, "Then we're going to be staying here in Oregon?"

"So it seems. Do you think I did the wrong thing?"

"No, I don't. But are we really ruined, too?"

"Lucinda, if I had a banker, that is probably what he would tell me."

"Do you suppose we Howards could go to Caralee's father and ask to borrow from his bank?"

"Good gracious, no. I haven't got any security to put down at all. He'd say no faster to me than he would to your Uncle Silas, and I gather that he didn't waste any time turning him down."

"But what if Aunt Adelina does well in her business and makes some money?"

"That might change matters, but it would take some time."

"Yes, ma'am." I left her room for mine with a heavy heart and threw myself onto my bed, where I lay scowling, watching the raindrops follow each other down my windowpane. Thunderation, things looked bad for everybody. I tried to fix my thoughts on bald-headed men, but couldn't keep my mind on that chore.

Supper was warmed-over goose and leftover potatoes and vegetables. There wasn't much said around the table, and afterward Aunt Adelina asked Henry Frederick for a favor. "Will you please go over to Mrs. Apley's house and ask her to come here tonight?"

"All right." He got up, put down his napkin, and before he put on his oilskins asked, "Are you going to tell her that

she can't work here anymore because we can't afford her?"
He didn't look to me as if he would enjoy the errand.

"Yes, that's part of what I want to talk to her about.
Also, please ask her to bring any eggshells she might not have
thrown out and any sulphur left over from last spring's
tonic for Zenobia and Yolanda."

"Sure, I'll remember. Sulphur and eggshells." That was
one thing about my brother. He'd lived so long with Aunt
Adelina that he wasn't much fazed by anything—except,
of course, by Mr. Whitlow's visits.

I did the supper dishes, wondering whether Uncle Silas
was getting anything to eat over at the Payday Saloon, which
gave free lunches but not free suppers. I was pouring boiling
water from the teakettle over the dishes as the last rinsing
when my brother came back with a box in his arms and
with Mrs. Apley and the two little girls following him
through the kitchen door.

Eleanora Apley, like her daughters, had yellowish-red
hair, slanting eyes, and a round, little body. She always
moved fast, and when she cleaned or got nervous or excited,
she talked with her hands, waving them about.

She seemed excited now as she unwound the blue scarf
from her head and took off her wet ulster, while the girls
shucked their oilskins and went to hang them up on the
back porch.

"Come, sit down, Eleanora," said my aunt, who sat alone
at the kitchen table, with her second cup of coffee in front
of her.

Mama had gone into the parlor, and Henry Frederick
followed her there once he'd put down the box by the big

black kitchen stove and got out of his rain clothing. What a climate the Willamette Valley had! If we'd all been given a silver dollar for every time it rained, there wouldn't be any talk of ruin! As it was, we put up with both ruin and rain!

I watched Mrs. Apley pour herself a cup of coffee from the pot on the stove and then sit down opposite my aunt. People in Oregon didn't stand on ceremony. Mrs. Apley had been born out West in California and that, according to Uncle Silas, explained her very independent nature.

Zenobia and Yolanda were already stationed in front of the cooky jar. My aunt told me, "Lucinda, give each of them a sugar cooky and then take them to the parlor and ask Henry Frederick to show them those stereopticon slides of Laplanders and reindeer." She asked the little girls, "Wouldn't you like to see the reindeer, my dears?"

"No," answered Zenobia. Yolanda, who was going on ten, caught tight hold of her hand, though, and said, "We'll go if we can have two cookies each and our ma says we can go."

"Your ma says that one cooky is enough, and you'd better go into the parlor right now and look at the reindeer, girls," said Mrs. Apley.

I stood by the door as the girls ran through it, cookie in hand, and asked, "Aunt Adelina, do I have to go into the parlor, too? Mama's already there to keep order."

"Not unless you want to, Lucinda. You seem to be deeply involved in what's going on already. This is what comes of drinking that wine New Year's Eve. Let it be a lesson to you about being an adult. When a child demands her rights

as a grown-up, she must take on the worries and responsi-
bilities of an adult, too."

"Amen to that," came from Mrs. Apley.

So I made up my mind to stay where I was, though I
dreaded hearing Mrs. Apley let go. I hoped she wouldn't
weep.

My aunt started in right away. "Eleanora, things have
taken a very bad turn here in Silas's business affairs. We
are going to have to cut back our expenses. We must take
in our belts severely."

Mrs. Apley nodded calmly, took a sip of coffee, and said,
"You don't have to come right out and say it, Missus Westlake. I've been feeling all autumn long that you were about
to tell me you couldn't keep me on. You've been a good
friend to me and mine. I understand your trouble."

"I'm sorry, Eleanora."

"It isn't your fault. It's the mister's fault the way I see it.
But I hear there's other men here in Denton who are in the
same boat. I hear people talking when I clean houses."

"There are other people ruined, too?" And then the idea
struck me that there must be, if other men were also turned
down at the bank today. I should have figured this out by
myself.

"Yep, Lucinda, ruined. It appears to me that quite a few
folks will be getting plaguey poor now and won't be able to
pay what they owe to Banker Lambertson. I'm glad I don't
owe anything to his bank. I've never even been inside it.
My pigs and my garden patch keep me going. Us Apleys
aren't high-living folks, but I have some small savings."

All at once my aunt shocked me by asking, "Eleanora,
would you lend me forty dollars in cash and give me that

sulphur Henry Frederick brought over on credit till I can pay you back?"

"Forty dollars? That's a heap of money, Missus Westlake."

"I promise you you'll get it back. In fact, you'll get more than your forty dollars. I'm going into business for myself. I'm going to make some preparations right here in my own kitchen and sell them here in Denton. If I'm successful I might even branch out. I think big! There are nearly one hundred thousand people in this state by now. I figure at least twenty thousand of them ought to be in deep need of what I plan to manufacture."

I saw Mrs. Apley's chin drop, and I could feel mine dropping, too. "Twenty thousand folks? What do they need beside a drier climate to keep the ache out of their bones?"

"Hair, Eleanora. Hair and pale complexions to make them feel beautiful and handsome."

"Hair?"

I explained, "We're going to make a hair restorer for bald-headed men and white powder for red-faced ladies."

My aunt said, "The eggshells you brought over just now are for the face powder, and the sulphur goes into the hair restorer. I need your forty dollars to buy ingredients for the cosmetics—rose water and orange extract and lots more sulphur. And I'll have to get jars and bottles from somewhere, so I can use any that you have to spare."

I saw Mrs. Apley's jaw tighten and her eyes start to shine. She set down her cup with a thud and exclaimed, "Rose water? Oh, Missus Westlake, I know of a wrinkle cream that uses rose water in it. It's got honey, white wax, and lily-bulb juice in it."

"A wrinkle cream?" My aunt frowned, staring at me, who

didn't have any wrinkles as yet. Then she said, "You know, I've been told of a hand cream that also uses melted white wax and oil of almonds. I wonder how much the wax costs?"

"Cheap. I'm sure it's cheap because candles are. All right, I'll give you forty dollars, and I'll help you cook up the things in the time I used to spend on housework here. I'll keep track of the hours I put in cooking for you, and you can pay me when you can. Aren't two kitchens cooking better than just one?"

Aunt Adelina smiled, then she sighed. "Oh, yes, two kitchens are—particularly when Silas doesn't approve of what I intend to do. You're a widow, Eleanora, so you can do whatever you choose without asking anyone's permission. If Silas's dinner is late two nights in a row because I've got some Hopi Hair Restorer cooking on the stove, he will tell me about it. And he might not take to the sulphur either, now that I come to think of it. He hates it when I'm making up the sulphur and molasses for Lucinda's and her brother's spring blood purifier."

"Yep, that sulphur stuff smells powerfully bad, Missus Westlake. Maybe I ought to make the things that have sulphur in them. My little gals can complain, but I can tell them to hush up."

"The sulphur is only in the hair restorer."

"Then I'll cook up that one, if you'll show me how. But who'll clean your house now that you're a working lady?" Mrs. Apley was leaning forward with both her elbows on the table.

"My sister Cassie says she will."

"How about Lucinda?" Mrs. Apley jerked her head toward me, making me sigh inside. I'd rather read or plunk on the organ than do housework. Who wouldn't?

My aunt rescued me. "No, Lucinda wants to help out in my business by going door to door selling my products. I'm sure her brother will do that for me, too. Cassie will take care of the house."

Then Mrs. Apley said, "I bet folks are going to find it interesting having Lucinda and Henry Fred come up to their doors."

I told her, "I'm already planning to make up a list of bald-headed men and red-faced ladies. Should I make up another one of wrinkle-faced ladies, Aunt Adelina?"

"You could do that, child. As I've told you, you and your brother should first deliver a leaflet to everyone on the list. Then you can come back the next day to take orders, and the day after that you will deliver the goods to them. As I see it, you need not say a single word to anyone unless you are asked to."

Mrs. Apley put in, "Should Lucinda go to the general store and to the drugstore, too, missus?"

"No, Eleanora, I have thought of those places and discarded them. I aim to make a quick profit. If I sell my cosmetics to stores, I would have to give up part of the profit to the storekeeper. Door to door is the cheapest to begin with. I think big, but I must start small."

"But, missus, Lucinda and Henry Fred have to go to school. They'll only be able to go out on Saturdays and after school, and they bring home homework, don't they?"

I answered her, "That's true, most always we do."

"Well, then," Mrs. Apley drew in her breath, grabbed hold of the edge of the tablecloth nearest her, crumpling it. and said, "it appears to me that you're going to need my Victor down here."

"Who is that?" asked my aunt.

"My dear boy."

"But I didn't know you had a son."

"Oh, yes, ma'am, he's been living up in Washington Territory with his pa's folks because I couldn't keep both him and the girls with me. Victor's been working. He's eighteen years old and out of school now. He'd be a mighty big help to you. I'd like to have him come down here, so I could get to know him before he goes farther away than Washington Territory."

"But I can't afford to pay a young man. I can't even afford to pay you, Eleanora."

"If I write Victor to come down and help me out in the hair-restorer business because I need him, I know that he'll come. And he won't ask for money until you can pay him. He won't mind the sulphur smell as long as he can be with his ma. My Victor could go door to door in the daytime. He's a jim-dandy of a seller. I hear tell he could sell a snow shovel to an Arab."

"All right, let him come then. It's up to you, Eleanora."

Mrs. Apley folded her arms across her chest. "You'll like Victor. Just you wait and see. And Zenobia and Yolanda are going to dote on their big brother."

Aunt Adelina asked the question I wanted to ask. "How does it happen that you have never spoken of Victor before?"

"Because I didn't want folks hereabouts blaming me for not keeping my son with me. I didn't want Victor to go away from me when my Abner died, but I couldn't support him because I had so little money. I had to give up quite a few things I used to take pleasure in after I lost my husband. Abner's folks offered to take Victor in and give him a home, so I let him go. It's a hard life being a widow who's got to go out and work to keep on living. I haven't been lucky enough to find a man that I would look at twice who wants to marry a widow with two little ones hanging onto her skirts."

I said, "Uncle Silas says that Mr. Gus Heffer wants to get married to somebody. He was just turned down by a widow in Kansas City."

Mrs. Apley sniffed. "That little bitty saloonkeeper, Lucinda?"

"Yes'm, the one who owns the Payday."

"Why he's so skinny you could pitch him through a flute. He ain't no fine figure of a man—not like my Abner was."

I told her, "I bet that's because he almost never gets a good meal." I didn't know whether Mr. Heffer did or not, but I thought she wasn't being very nice to him. "I think he's more to be pitied than censured." It was a saying Mama favored.

"Fah, Lucinda." Mrs. Apley was hardhearted toward Mr. Heffer. "He probably drinks his dinner. All that matters in the world to that sort of man comes in bottles."

"Be charitable, Eleanora," said my aunt. "Heffer is getting bald."

*   *   *

Four days later my hard-working aunt, with Mama's help, had made up some small, handwritten leaflets advertising the Hopi Hair Restorer, Magnolia Milk Face Powder, and what she and Mrs. Apley had decided to call Persian Pool Hand Soother and Lady Elinor's Anti-Time Cream.

I'd worked hard on my three lists. After asking Aunt Adelina, Mama, and Mrs. Apley for ladies' names, I had put down forty-two wrinkled ones and thirty with red noses or chins. Some of the unfortunate ladies had both of these troubles. I didn't have any list for rough-handed folks because nobody seemed to notice other people's hands. However, the hand-soother cream was advertised on the same leaflet with the wrinkle cream. Maybe because a man's bald head was something everybody really took heed of—even if it was commonly found—there were nearly a hundred names on that special list.

So, after school, on the night of January 5, Henry Frederick and I went out separately. He took the papers for the face powder and wrinkle cream because ladies always kept telling Mama, in his hearing, how handsome he was. When I was little, gentlemen used to pat me on the head and call me "little dear," so I took the leaflets about the hair restorer to the men.

Everytime I went into an office or store in town selling hair restorer and asked for the man of the place, I planned to hand him one of the leaflets, then wait for him to read it and tell me to come back tomorrow and take his order.

Things didn't work out quite the way I'd expected them to, though. Most of the bald or balding men didn't seem very eager to take the leaflet. I supposed after a while that they simply didn't like taking papers from people.

For a fact, just about every one of the men asked me rather suspiciously, "What are you selling?"

Then I'd have to say, "My aunt, Mrs. Silas Westlake, makes something that'll make the hair grow on top of your head real quick again."

Generally, the man I was talking to would answer, "Oh, she does, does she?" And he would stare at me.

While he was staring at me, I'd stick the leaflet into his hand or on his counter or desk and say, "Fine, I'll be back tomorrow to take your order for the hair restorer." And then I'd curtsey and leave.

It was different when I ran into ladies at the front doors of houses. Those times I'd smile at her and give her a paper and say right out, "This is what my aunt, Mrs. Silas Westlake, thinks will help the man who lives here to grow his hair back. Maybe you'll want to buy the hair restorer as a present for him."

The ladies didn't stare. Mostly they looked surprised. A couple of them smiled as they started to read the leaflet I gave them. I thought they must have been pleased to think that somebody in their own town had found the secret for growing hair on their menfolk's heads again.

And that's pretty much how it went that afternoon in Denton. I went to as many places as I could before it started getting dark, though not to saloons, where I was forbidden to enter. After I was through for the day, I couldn't help but think that some men had reacted queerly. I thought I understood why. They were amazed to learn that there was such a thing as a hair restorer being made right here in little Denton. I noticed how Banker Lambertson had stared at me when he'd opened the bank door to let me in after hours and let me out again, after I'd given him a paper about the hair restorer. He'd shut the door behind me and bolted it. I'd heard the bolt being pushed across the door and felt a little like a bank robber.

I found my brother at our rendezvous, standing under a pine tree, taking shelter from the rain. He must have gotten around Denton faster than I had, or he'd said less to the future lady customers than I had to the men. Then, too, the lists of wrinkled and red-nosed ladies had been shorter.

I asked him, "What did you say to the ladies you delivered the papers to? Did you have to talk to them?"

"Yep, most of them asked me what I was selling before they'd even take a paper. When a wrinkled-up one asked me what the paper was about, I'd say, "My aunt, who's Mrs. Silas Westlake, thinks you might like this here wrinkle cream she's making. You can read all about it on this paper. I'll come back tomorrow to take your order."

I nodded because he'd said the right thing. "All right, what did you say to the red-nosed ones if one of them came to the door and didn't want to take a leaflet?"

"Oh, I told them, 'Please read this paper. Use this here powder on your nose and cheeks that my aunt, Mrs. Westlake, is making. It'll take the red color out of your face better than throwing a teaspoonful of gin and warm water on it.' "

"Thunderation, Henry Frederick, where did you ever hear about that?"

"Uncle Silas told me a long time ago that some ladies he used to know back East did that to get rid of red blotches on their face."

I scolded him. "You shouldn't have told these Oregon ladies that. It might be cheaper than buying the face powder. Aunt Adelina's really pounding up the eggshells these days, you know."

He stood his ground and said, "Lucinda, I don't think the ladies here want to use gin because I think they're smart enough to know that Aunt Adelina's face powder will smell a whole lot better."

As we walked home together, I said, "It will be interesting to see how many orders we get, won't it?"

"Uh-huh, I really worked hard today. I ran from house to house. Come on, let's get home and dry out," he said, as he waded right through a puddle in his rubber boots, the way he always did.

CHAPTER IV

A Door-to-Door Lesson

I thought things were extremely strange when we went out the next afternoon to take orders.

Only thirty-four of the men I'd given leaflets to ordered bottles of Hopi Hair Restorer, and a couple of them rather rudely told me that they doubted if it would be worth what Aunt Adelina was charging for it. Some others said they were old customers of Uncle Silas's from his sawmill days and because of that they didn't have any hard feelings against the Westlakes, but they still weren't going to buy tonic from me. Some other men either walked away from me when I came into their stores and offices or banged shut their front doors when they saw me coming along the boardwalk. Banker Lambertson said no to me through the bank window, which he closed right afterward. Another Denton man pulled down the blind of his office window, and I heard the door lock as I grabbed his doorknob. A couple of the bald men I'd visited yesterday were wearing hats and caps when I came to take their orders, even though they were inside buildings.

Henry Frederick was waiting for me at the same spot at dusk, but today he seemed more down in the mouth than yesterday. I told him what had happened to me, then said, "I just don't understand it. I only got thirty-four orders in all for the hair grower. I hope you did lots better with the ladies you saw."

He scowled at me. "I sure saw a lot of ladies, but I only got nine orders for the wrinkle cream and twenty-nine for the hand soother."

I said, "What about the Magnolia Milk Face Powder?"

"I only got three orders for that, Lucinda."

I thought I could understand that all right. "That's because you had to tell them all about that teaspoonful-of-gin-in-water trick."

"Maybe you're right. That might be why they didn't want the powder. Of course, today I didn't get to talk to every one of the ladies I saw yesterday. Some of them either were sick or weren't at home. When they didn't come to the front door, I always went around to try the back one in case they were in the kitchen. But nobody came there either."

I said, "Aunt Adelina and Mrs. Apley aren't going to like this. I guess they'll have to go to the emporium and to the drugstore and ask the owners to sell their things for them. I know they don't want to, but I don't see any other way. Door-to-door selling just doesn't work in Denton."

He told me, "Not unless Victor Apley can do better than we can."

As my brother and I walked home together in a drizzle that matched our moods, we talked about the Westlakes. Things weren't good between the two of them at all. Uncle Silas, who used to sit in the parlor and read from his books of essays once he'd finished the Portland *Oregonian*, spent most of his time out in the carriage house now. He'd sold the bay horse that used to pull the rig but not the rig itself. With the rig still in there, the carriage house was pretty crowded, with his rolltop desk, chairs, bench, hat rack, and business ledgers.

I didn't go out there, but Henry Frederick did. It appeared to me from the queer looks my uncle gave me now and then that he had the idea that I was on Aunt Adelina's side and, therefore, against him. That wasn't so. It wasn't that I was so much on her side, but I did think that she ought to have the chance to prove that she could do something to make money if she wanted to. Silas had had lots of opportunities to do many things. All Aunt Adelina had been able to do since she'd married him was to keep house for him.

When Henry Frederick and I got home, Mama told us that Aunt Adelina was over at Mrs. Apley's, showing her how to make the Hopi Hair Restorer. So, without taking off our raincoats, we walked the quarter mile or so to the little gray house on Sycamore Street.

We could smell the hair restorer cooking before we even got to the house. I supposed that stink had to be the sulphur. I surely hoped that the whole top of the Apley stove wasn't covered with pots of the restorer—not when I had orders for only thirty-four bottles.

Zenobia opened the door for us and said, "Victor's here."

I told her, "That was pretty fast, wasn't it?"

"Yes, Ma sent him a telegram. He came down right off." She grabbed me by the hand. "Come on, I'll show you my big brother."

There was a long-legged, thin, young man with straw-colored hair straddling one of the kitchen chairs, leaning his head on his arms. He was watching his mother and our aunt stirring two big, blue-speckled pots without helping them; he was just sitting and grinning. Dressed in brown-striped trousers and a yellow vest and a big, flowing, brown-silk tie, he looked snappy, all right.

"This here's Lucinda and her brother, Henry Fred," Zenobia told Victor, letting go of my hand and lolling on him. Yolanda was lolling over him on his other side.

Victor had a high voice and spoke fast. "Pleased to make your acquaintance, I'm sure." Then he yawned and stretched. My, but he was long-armed.

Well, I wasn't exactly delighted to make his acquaintance. I thought he was rude because he didn't get up when I came into the Apley kitchen. After all I was thirteen and gentlemen who were gentlemen, particularly gentlemen hosts, stood up for ladies. So all I said was, "Hello. I never heard of you before the other day."

He put his finger to his lips. "Oh, I'm just one of Ma's little secrets."

"You hush up, Victor," commanded Mrs. Apley, turning away from the stove with a dripping wooden spoon in her hand. It was stained bright yellow. Sulphur all right.

He laughed, then said, "Sure, Ma, I'll hush up."

How she beamed at him! Her smile went all the way across her face. It was plain to see that she doted on him.

Aunt Adelina turned her head to look over her shoulder at Henry Frederick and me for a moment. Before she went back to her stirring, she said, "Sit down. I'll talk to you in a minute or so. We have to get the sugar and lead and sulphur well mixed before we put in the rose water." She coughed because of the sulphur fumes and went back to her stirring.

Henry Frederick whispered to me, "They should have started with the rose water and put in that smelly yellow stuff later on. It would smell better now that way." He put his fingers onto his nose.

Lead? I couldn't believe it. I whispered to Henry Frederick over the racket of the spoons against the sides of the pots. "I didn't know they were going to put lead into the restorer. I know lead melts down, but do you think anybody would want to put lead on his head?"

My brother, who hadn't heard my whisper asked out loud, "Aunt Adelina, you don't have to turn around to answer me, but does a man drink the Hopi Hair Restorer or does he put it on his head?"

Victor Apley grabbed his two little sisters around their waists, leaned back in his chair, and roared with laughter. Before Aunt Adelina could answer, he cried, "Lead's a deadly poison, little boy. This stuff goes on top of the head, of course."

The way he was treating Henry Frederick made me see red. So I said, "Victor Apley, we both know that, of course. Henry Frederick was only joshing with Aunt Adelina." I moved over to my brother fast and stepped on his foot the way I sometimes did to let him know not to say anything more. I wasn't going to have us Howards shamed in front of this fellow from Washington Territory.

I looked at the kitchen table, which was covered with just-washed bottles with the labels scrubbed off. Some of them looked familiar. We'd sorted through all of the bottles and jars in our woodshed and brought them over here. They were all sizes, shapes, and colors. I counted them while the ladies stirred and Victor hummed "Pretty Star of the Night" to his sisters. As for my brother, he stood his ground, glaring at Victor Apley.

When I'd finished counting, I sighed. "Aunt Adelina, I counted seventy-two bottles here. You've got lots more than you're going to need. I only took orders for thirty-four."

"Thirty-four? Is that *all*?" She whirled around with a look of dismay on her face and her spoon dripping yellow goo all the way down the front of her apron. "But there are well over a hundred men who could use the hair restorer in Denton."

"Yes'm, but there are only thirty-four who want it."

"Eleanora, stop!" Aunt Adelina grabbed hold of Mrs. Apley's arm just as Mrs. Apley reached for the jug of rose water on the floor beside the stove. "Eleanora, don't put any of that into the pots yet, please. Could you stir both pots for me while I talk to Lucinda and Henry Frederick. This is important."

"Sure, but first I'll push the pots closer together to make it easier, and then you give me your spoon, too."

While Mrs. Apley stirred with her left and her right hand, Aunt Adelina came to stand before me and my brother.

Victor was watching us the way a cat watches a mousehole in the wall.

Our aunt exploded, "I can't believe it. You should have three times as many orders for the hair restorer. How did you do on the orders for the face powder and other things?"

My brother said, "Oh, I took the orders for them. I got nine for the wrinkle cream and twenty-nine for the hand soother."

"Only nine for the anti-time cream?" She was shocked all over again.

"That's all, Aunt Adelina. It gets worse, though, when it comes to the face powder. There's only three ladies interested in buying that."

"My word, but this is dreadful!" She sank down in a chair across from Victor Apley and his lolling little sisters.

I was glad to have Victor speak up next, because I was worried that Henry Frederick would blurt out what he had said to customers about the gin and lukewarm water. I didn't want him to shame himself again.

Victor said, "Lemme see if I heard you two kids right? The girl here went out and took the orders from the gents for the hair restorer, and the boy took them for the creams and the powder, the items lady customers would be buying for themselves?"

"That's right," I told him.

He didn't look at me but at Aunt Adelina. "That was wrong." Then he looked at me and asked, "Whose idea was it to do things that way?"

Aunt Adelina replied to him, "It got rather mixed up, it seems. I told the children to say as little as possible—just take the orders and say something only when they were asked to. Nearly everybody in town knows Lucinda and Henry Frederick."

Victor had a frown on his face. "You can be danged sure if they didn't know them before, they know them now. I bet they know them all too well." He was eyeing my brother and me some more. "Tell me, how did you two kids go about getting the orders and just what did you say to customers?"

"Do I have to tell him?" I asked Aunt Adelina. I didn't take one bit to Victor Apley.

"Please do, Lucinda. Something seems to have gone very wrong somewhere."

She was staring at the empty bottles, which would probably never get filled now, and I could tell that she wasn't one bit happy.

So, in spite of the fact that I didn't want to, I told them what I'd done and what I'd said.

By the time I'd finished, Victor had pushed his sisters away and had one hand over his brow. "Oh, no," he moaned, "she even stared at their bald heads."

I defended myself. "I had to do that. I wasn't going to try to sell hair restorer to a man who had a lot of hair. What if I had the wrong name and was making a mistake?"

Victor moaned again.

Henry Frederick's turn came next. Shifting his weight from one foot to the other, he told Aunt Adelina what he'd said to the ladies, but not the part about the gin and warm water. Leaving that out made me feel better. He made it sound as if he'd only let them know that the face powder would take the red out of their faces.

By the time Henry Frederick was done, Victor Apley had

his hands up over his face. "It gets worse and worse." All at once he took his hands down, and while his mother went on stirring he told our aunt, "Mrs. Westlake, I think you'd better give up the idea of selling these things in Denton at all now. It won't work. Even if you're able to place the merchandise in the local stores, the items aren't going to sell. Your niece and nephew have seen to that." He looked at Henry Frederick and me and shook his head. "I know you two meant well, but you kids probably made the whole town mad at your family. They'll get over that in time, but they won't ever do much buying."

Thunderation, I didn't like hearing that. Before Aunt Adelina could speak up, I flared at him, "Well, if you're so all-fired smart, Victor Apley, how *should* we have done it?"

He stuck a finger out at me, and I longed to bite it. Then he said, "You, Lucy, should have gone to see the ladies and handed them each one of the leaflets and left at once without speaking one single word. Your brother should have visited the gents and done the same thing. Folks like to buy things that are personal from folks of the same sex."

"Well, you are probably correct in that," Aunt Adelina agreed. "What do you suggest that I do now?"

I wanted to hear what he'd say. He seemed to think he was a real jim-dandy when it came to selling things to people, and maybe he did know a thing or two. His mother had claimed he could sell a snow shovel to an Arab.

He told our aunt, "Make up the bottles the kids took orders for and maybe ten or so extra ones. Deliver the goods to the customers, and store what you have left over in case somebody likes your products and wants to buy some more from you. If anybody does, that person can come to your house and get more. But whatever you do, don't send these two kids out on their own again!"

Aunt Adelina said, "Oh dear, what will Silas say to this? He won't know whether to laugh or to cry. The way I have it figured right now we won't be making a nickel. We'll only break even on the cost of the materials."

"It could be worse, Mrs. Westlake," said Victor, whom I had to admit did seem to have good sense about selling. Besides, I hadn't truly enjoyed going door to door.

In a way Victor Apley could be looked upon as my rescuer.

"How could it be worse, Victor?" asked his mother.

"You two ladies could have lost money."

"Yes, I imagine that's so," said Aunt Adelina, with a small groan. "Well, Eleanora, it doesn't seem that we were in business for long, does it?"

"No, missus, we were in quick and out quicker."

Victor nodded. "That's how it seems to be here in Denton at least. But Mrs. Westlake, don't you or Ma throw away the formulas for the cosmetics. Maybe when I get more established in life, I can find somebody who'd want to buy them. Keep watch here in Denton, and see what folks have to say about the things you're making. Great Scott, ladies, if that Indian hair restorer makes new hair on a bald man's head, the whole world ought to know about it. Does it do that, Mrs. Westlake?"

"It grew some fuzz on my great-uncle's head back in Pennsylvania."

"Fuzz probably doesn't count, does it, Victor?" asked Mrs. Apley.

"No, Ma, fuzz doesn't."

Aunt Adelina had been sitting with her lips compressed

tightly together. "Well, we aren't licked yet, Eleanora. This is just a temporary setback, I hope. There is still Mr. Bradshaw's tonic."

"What's that?" asked Victor.

"The Tuscarora Tonic. That could possibly be the answer to my prayers."

The instant after my aunt had said these hopeful words there came a very loud bang from the side of the Apleys' rolltop kitchen cabinet.

Yolanda cried, "Ma, your baking-powder can has fallen down again."

"Ah," I heard my aunt say very softly.

"It's all right. You won't need to get the kitchen stool, Yolanda," said Victor, who finally got up. He went to the cabinet across the kitchen, opened the top of it, and peeked inside. Then he said, "Nope, the baking powder didn't fall down, Yolanda."

I looked at Henry Frederick, who was staring wide-eyed at me. Mr. Whitlow here? Thunderation! He came calling wherever our aunt went. I surely hoped Aunt Adelina wouldn't say what she thought the banging sound really was. Oh, she'd seemed tickled to hear it. She was even smiling now.

Victor went back to his chair and sat down. "Mrs. Westlake, why don't you let me have a look at that formula you've got?" he asked.

"No." She shook her head. "It's a secret formula."

He asked, "Do you know anything about that kind of thing? They can be mighty tricky, I hear tell. I take it that what you've got is a herb remedy?"

She nodded. "In a way it is, and in a way it isn't. My

father was an apothecary, and my grandmother was known far and wide as an herb woman. Yes, I know something about herbs and about the other things that would go into a tonic, I suppose."

"What things, Mrs. Westlake?" Victor surely had a curiosity bump.

"Just some weeds from the wilderness. Just some Oregon weeds that won't be found in tonics sold in other parts of the land. I plan to add a few items here and there to the Bradshaw formula."

"Well, that is very interesting." Victor was looking thoughtful, it seemed to me, as he reached out to play with one of Zenobia's long braids, now that she had come back to loll on him some more. He started to whistle the same tune again.

I asked Aunt Adelina, "Can we go home now? My feet are tired, and they're cold in these rubber boots from walking in the rain so much today."

"Surely, but first leave the merchandise orders you took with Eleanora and me."

"I will." I fished the damp hair-restorer list out of my pocket and gave it to her. Henry Frederick's lists were even soggier, but she could make out the names in pencil on them. We'd both used our best penmanship, even if we hadn't said the right things to people, according to Victor Apley.

I asked, "Aunt Adelina, do you expect Henry Frederick and me to deliver the jars and bottles when you're ready?"

"No, Lucinda. Victor will do that for us. It will be a good way for him to get to know Denton before he starts looking for work in earnest here."

That suited me just fine, and I was sure it was dandy with Henry Frederick, too. "Let Victor do it" was my motto of the moment.

On our way back home, my brother said something I felt like hitting him over the head for. "You ought to ask Aunt Adelina to give you some of her mashed-up eggshell powder to use on your face the next time it gets so red."

I stopped in my tracks. "When did my face get red?"

"When that old Victor told you you didn't know how to sell merchandise."

"Well, maybe I did blush a little, but you got plenty red when he said the same thing about you."

"I didn't blush like you. Boys don't—not in the face. Only on the tops of their ears sometimes."

"Thunderation, Henry Frederick Howard!" were my only words to that.

And then it did thunder. Right overhead came a great big clap of it. I said, "Well, that was natural, wasn't it?"

My brother understood me. "Yep, that wasn't Mr. Whitlow this time," he said.

I had to admire Aunt Adelina even more for what happened that night after supper. She came right out with it and told Uncle Silas that they had "failed" in the cosmetic business. And she didn't tell him that it was our fault, which made her even more admirable to my way of thinking. I was more than ever on her side and was hoping she'd find a way to rescue us from being ruined.

Henry Frederick failed me, though, when I told him how much I admired our aunt for her honesty, even though

Uncle Silas had looked sour and had sighed. My brother told me, "Don't give her so much credit for that, Lucinda. If she hadn't told Uncle Silas, I was going to tell him. Uncle Silas and I are sticking together now more than before. I don't aim to sell any more things."

"You do that, Henry Frederick. Go on and desert Aunt Adelina and Mama and me. Go on, we don't need you. We don't need *any* man."

"What about old Mr. Whitlow?" And off he sashayed to the carriage house, proud of having gotten in the last word, something that rarely happened between the two of us.

My brother seemed to spend more and more time out in the carriage house with Uncle Silas in the next week. That wasn't only because he and I had had words or that Aunt Adelina was smashing up eggshells and the kitchen smelled of rose-water perfume. It was because Victor Apley was around so much. He was almost always in our kitchen, talking to our aunt, when we came home from school. Whenever I hung around to hear what he was saying, he seemed to be asking her something about the Tuscarora Tonic. He'd delivered the hair restorer and the other bottles of things and got some more orders for the face powder, which explained the work on the eggshells. But he never seemed to be talking about cosmetics with Aunt Adelina.

I couldn't understand why she let him loll around her so, but I decided not to ask her because these days she was inclined to be quite snappish. Because I was grown-up now and I hadn't done so well selling things door to door, I was trying to think the way I thought adults would think. It wasn't easy, and it appeared to me that most of the things they thought about weren't very pleasant. They seemed to worry about money more than anything else. Right now my aunt was worried about money, Uncle Silas, and the future. And she was certainly pinching the pennies. We were eating a lot of dried beans and peas and home-canned fruits, meats, and vegetables. She'd gotten some little pigs from a farmer's wife she knew, so now we had six pigs, not just one. What we didn't eat, the pigs did.

Finally, toward the end of that January, I asked Mama about Victor's hanging around so much and she told me, "Your aunt wants to keep in touch with him. She has been told that he could be useful to her."

"Told? Who by?"

Mama pointed to the cottage organ.

"Mr. Whitlow?" That was who, of course, but I asked the question all the same.

"No, Lucinda." Mama pursed her lips over her crocheting. "Not him—not this time. Adelina claims it was one of her tribe of Indians. The Indians in the spirit world are taking notice of her troubles because of the Tuscarora Tonic."

I snorted and said, "They weren't much help to her on the Hopi Hair Restorer, were they? And neither was Mr. Whitlow."

I heard Mama laugh now for the first time in days.

On the first Saturday in February Aunt Adelina asked me to come walking with her in the woods. She told me, "Lucinda, I plan to make fern pie for supper. Bring the basket you use to gather dandelion blossoms."

"Fern pie?" It didn't sound tasty to me, but I supposed she knew what she was up to. She usually did.

She had a big basket and a trowel and shovel. When we'd crawled under a farmer's fence, gone through his cherry orchard, and crossed a meadow of wet, high grass, we went into dark woods of cedar and hemlock trees at the edge of the farm a long ways from the farmhouse.

She showed me how to cut off the stalks of the young, pale-green ferns for the pie. While we did that, keeping our eyes peeled for black bears and cougars, she talked to me about the things you could find in the wilderness to eat.

I'd already known about huckleberries and the salmon trout in the Willamette River and about deer because we ate a lot of venison and venison mincemeat. Uncle Silas was a good fisherman and not a bad hunter with a rifle. I'd heard, too, about the Indians eating camas bulbs, though I'd never tried one.

But the things she knew were a surprise to me—and very interesting to boot. She told me, "Lucinda, Oregon is a wonderful place in spite of the rain. When you can see them through the mists, the hills and mountains out here are magnificent. I love these woods in the springtime when the dogwood and syringa are in bloom."

I agreed. I liked to see them, but I liked the little yellow violets and white trilliums even more. They grew in the deepest, darkest places. The meadows were bright with yellow buttercups and blue with wild flag in summer, but still I liked the spring wild flowers best of all.

When Aunt Adelina and I had cut enough ferns, she said, "Come along, my dear, we have other things to get today. I didn't come out here just for ferns. I want some roots of Chinook licorice and wild poppy and some dogwood bark. I'll look around for them, if you'll dig up some roots of Oregon grape plants for me. I take it you know an Oregon grape when you see one?"

"Sure I do. It's easy. It's common everywhere."

All at once she asked, "All right, tell me why it's useful."

This stopped me. I stood in the dripping forest, shaking my head.

"It's a medicine, a tonic, Lucinda."

I cried, "Oh, you're really going to make Mr. Bradshaw's old tonic then?"

"Perhaps I'll have a stab at it and, as I have said, make some changes in it. I plan to brew up a batch just for the sake of the health and well-being of the five of us, you understand. I don't like our diet these days. It isn't as good and healthful as it once was, now that we no longer buy beef and lamb and eat only chicken because the pigs are too young to slaughter. I believe we should all take a good bracing tonic this spring, as usual, and because that tonic I've been buying costs an arm and a leg these days, I think I will make my own this year."

"I hope the one you make tastes better than the one you used to buy."

She grinned at me as I came to a halt in front of a little, shiny-leaved Oregon grape bush growing under a madrona tree. "That's right, Lucinda. That's Oregon grape. I must tell you about medicines, though. Let it be a lesson to you. If a medicine tastes pleasant, most people will think it won't do them any good. If it tastes too good, they'll think it's a syrup and take too much of it."

"But if it tastes too bad, they won't take it at all," I added.

"Well, what a person must aim at then is a not-too-pleasant medicine."

"I suppose that's so." I knelt down beside the bush and tried to pull it up out of the rain-soaked ground by brute force. It wouldn't come. While I dug it out with the trowel, I could hear my aunt breaking her way through the underbrush with her basket and the shovel.

Spring tonic. At the very thought of it I made a sour face.

The fern pie Aunt Adelina made with eggs from our hen house and served with cornmeal biscuits and honey was very good. In fact, I thought it was good enough to have over again, so after supper I volunteered to go out with her in the woods for more ferns.

But she replied, "No." Then she added, "You and Henry Frederick can go if your mother will give her permission. You know how to select the ferns, Lucinda. I have some things I must do here in the house from now on. I'll dry the roots we got today overnight in a slow oven. Tomorrow I plan to purchase some dry herbs from the druggist with some of Mrs. Apley's money, which she refuses to take back. The herbs are very expensive. I think I may go up to Portland on the new train before long on an errand, but before I do that we must have Mr. Heffer over for supper."

"Gus Heffer?" I heard the name spoken, then heard Uncle Silas's spoon drop with a thud on the top of the dinner table. He hadn't paid any real attention to what she'd said about the ferns and herbs and neither had Henry Frederick, but this news startled both of them.

"Yes, Silas, Mr. Heffer. You heard me correctly. As I

recall, you once said we should be more friendly toward him. I think we should have him over for a meal along with the Apley family."

"Why, Adelina?" I thought my uncle looked suspicious.

"For a most noble and selfless reason. I have been thinking lately about poor little Eleanora Apley, who has just yesterday lost another one of her housecleaning jobs because the family also owes the Denton Bank. Victor is one more hungry mouth for her to feed. Victor needs work, and Mr. Heffer has a prosperous saloon, which needs to be swept out now and then, I presume. I presume, too, that there are other chores there that Victor could perform. He is a strong youth and ambitious."

"Is that all, Adelina?" came from Uncle Silas.

"Not quite, my dear. Mrs. Apley needs a husband. Mr. Heffer needs a wife. They are the right age for one another. Zenobia and Yolanda need a father's guidance badly, and it is well known that Gus Heffer dotes on little girls and hands out peppermint sticks to them when they pass the Payday Saloon on their way home from church."

"Hmm," was our uncle's only comment.

"And there is one other thing, Silas. There is the matter of Willard."

I asked, "Who's that?"

"Willard Apley. Eleanora told me about him last night. He's her second son."

Uncle Silas demanded, "*Second* son? Where does *he* live?"

"In Idaho Territory with a cousin of Mr. Apley's. She wrote the cousin that Victor was here, and the cousin wrote back that he thinks Willard should come to Oregon to get to know his mother, too. Once Eleanora gets Victor settled at work, she says it would make her very happy to have Willard with her and the girls."

Mama wanted to know, "Does anybody else here in Denton know about Willard?"

"No, no one knows but the five of us at this table and the Apley family. I think it would be a noble gesture for us to introduce Mr. Heffer and Mrs. Apley to one another. Don't you agree, Silas? Heffer could solve the problem of Victor neatly."

"Poor little—" was all Uncle Silas said. I didn't quite catch the word after *little*. It might have been *cuss*, or it might have been *Gus*. I wondered if he'd been muttering about Mr. Heffer or about Victor, but I didn't dare ask.

CHAPTER V

"Thunderation, That's a Mouthful!"

That night I asked Mama privately what she knew about Mr. Heffer's being asked to supper. She told me that she didn't really understand why Aunt Adelina was suddenly being so friendly toward him, though it was noble of her to want to help her friend Mrs. Apley. She thought it was strange, too, that she'd be asking a saloonkeeper to our house.

Naturally, I told Caralee the news. She was so surprised that she stepped into a mud puddle in the school yard. While she shook the mud and water off her boot, she exclaimed, "But, Lucinda, he's a saloonkeeper!"

"I know, but Uncle Silas and Aunt Adelina think he'd make a good husband for Mrs. Apley, who needs one now that she's getting the rest of her family around her."

97

"Oh, you mean that old Victor? I saw him at my uncle's house when he came to deliver hand cream to my aunt." She made a face. "He acts as if he's running for mayor. That's what my mama says. She saw him that day, too."

"He isn't any good friend of mine, Caralee."

She was frowning as we walked back to the small white schoolhouse, after Miss Hinkle had come out on the front porch to ring the hand bell. While we threaded our way through all the yelling little kids, running and splashing through puddles on their way inside, she told me, "My mama says that matchmaking is one of the most dangerous things anybody can do. She says it can blow up in a person's face. A matchmaker can start out with two friends and end up with two foes. Besides, Mrs. Apley used to be a servant of your aunt's, didn't she? And she's coming to your house for supper?"

Because I didn't like snobbishness, I said, "Well, Mrs. Apley doesn't work for the Westlakes anymore. She's Aunt Adelina's partner in business. We aren't snobs like some Denton folks I could put names to."

"I suppose you mean Papa and Mama and me?" That had got her goat all right.

"If the shoe fits, put it on, Caralee Lambertson. And I might add—*rich* snobs."

She whirled around, putting the back of her umbrella between us and said in a cold tone, "My papa says he'd like me to stop being friends with you, Lucinda Lavina Howard. In the first place, we do think your aunt is quite peculiar. He says you have become a rude child, who should not be let out of doors unless you are on a chain. He didn't like it one bit when you came sashaying into his bank to give him that dreadful leaflet about that old Indian hair grower. Mama thought that was perfectly horrible of you, too. And so do I. My papa can't help being almost bald."

I said to the spike of her umbrella, which was poking into my cheek, "And I can't help it that my Uncle Silas is ruined, but your pa could help if he wanted to."

"Good-bye to you, Lucinda." And she hurried up the school steps ahead of me, leaving me glaring down below, muttering to myself about, among other things, what snobs the Lambertsons were.

Perhaps I hadn't made things easier for Aunt Adelina by staring at Banker Lambertson's head, which glistened on the top like a peeled onion. He surely kept it spotlessly clean. Maybe he had it in for us now because of what I'd done.

I was still muttering as I passed the teacher. "I hope old Mr. Lambertson loses the hair fringes along the side of his head, too. Even if he should beg me on bended knee for a sip of the spring tonic Aunt Adelina's going to make for us, I won't give him one. Not even if he's got boils all over and his teeth are getting so long he can't shut his mouth anymore."

"What are you muttering about, Lucinda?" asked Miss Hinkle, who was youngish and pretty as well as educated.

"Nothing, I was just thinking about weeds."

She nodded. "Oh, yes, botany is a very interesting subject. You should study it when you go on to high school."

"I'm already studying it." I wanted to add that I didn't know if I ever would get to high school.

I'd faced that possibility, too. Maybe I would have to go to work clerking in a store, if I could find work in a year as bad as this one. That's what a lot of the kids did after the

eighth grade. Not everyone got to go on to high school. The high school here was Denton Academy, a private school, like many in the United States. It cost thirty-five dollars a year for tuition, and the way things looked we wouldn't be able to spare that much money. Someday secondary school might be free the way grammar school was. But by that time Henry Frederick and I would be too old.

I'd looked forward to going to Denton Academy, even if it meant going to school six days a week, six hours a day, and taking Latin and Greek, as well as algebra and botany. Caralee was going. So were some of my other girl friends who were eighth graders now.

People in Oregon believed in education and in educating females. There were colleges in the Willamette Valley, although the state wasn't twenty years old yet. According to Uncle Silas, Oregon folks, Westerners, were firm believers in "progress."

I also believed in progress. It seemed to me that inasmuch as the hair restorer and eggshell powder had been failures, somebody ought to get cracking on something that would be a real money-maker.

As I sat down at the desk I shared with Caralee, I knew I'd have to speak to her one more time today. I leaned over and said, "I am threatening you now. If you tell anybody that we want Mr. Heffer to marry Mrs. Apley, I'll let all your chickens out of their coop and all your rabbits out of their hutches. If you had beehives, I'd turn them over, too."

She gave me a look that would have curdled new milk, then whispered, "You don't have to worry. I don't ever speak the names of saloonkeepers and house servants aloud."

Because Miss Hinkle was back at her desk, looking over her schoolroom and watching for whisperers, all I could do was make a horrible face at my once-upon-a-time best friend from behind my spelling book.

After school, Caralee tried to get in the last word by asking me outside the schoolhouse, "What does your crazy aunt's Mr. Whitlow have to say these days?"

"Plenty, Caralee Lambertson! Plenty, you bet!" And then I turned around and started for home.

Henry Frederick soon came slopping along to catch up with me. He asked, "Did you have a fight with Caralee?"

"Yes, I did."

"What did you fight about?"

"Mrs. Apley and Mr. Heffer and her papa's bald head and Aunt Adelina and Mr. Whitlow."

"Him, too?" He whistled through the gap in his front teeth.

"Yes, him, too. The fight I had with her was a bad one this time. We won't be friends from now on. I told her the Lambertsons were snobs, rich ones."

"Are you going to tell Mama or the Westlakes what you quarreled about?"

"No." I frowned. I'd thought about that all afternoon while I'd been taking a hard test in long division. "It would upset Uncle Silas and Aunt Adelina to hear that Banker Lambertson may be down on them because of my staring at his head. They have to keep their minds on the money they owe his bank. I don't want them to get the idea that there's something private and personal between Lambertson and us now." I sighed. "Maybe I'll put on some of Aunt

Adelina's anti-time cream tonight. This is the kind of thing that gives a lady wrinkles in a rush."

He told me, "Maybe it's a good thing you didn't take a leaflet to Mr. Heffer at the Payday Saloon, Lucinda."

I hated to say it, but I did. "I think you're right."

As usual, because of our wet rain clothes we went inside the house through the kitchen door. After being scolded plenty of times, we'd learned to hang our oilskins on pegs to drip where the rainwater didn't cause any damage.

But today there was a handwritten sign pinned on the back door that read:

Woman at Work
Keep Out, Please

"What does that mean?" Henry Frederick asked me.

"It means that we have to go around to the front door. Aunt Adelina put that up to keep folks out."

We went through the dripping grass to the front door and came in that way. Mama was playing softly on the cottage organ. After we'd hung our oilskins in the front hall over basins that had been set out for them to drip into, I went in to speak to her. She put her finger to her lips and went on playing with one hand.

"Don't upset your aunt, children. She's out in the kitchen struggling with the formula Mr. Bradshaw gave your uncle."

I asked, "Where's Uncle Silas?"

"He's in Denton trying to sell the carriage and whatever else anybody will buy. Then he's going over to the Payday Saloon and ask Mr. Heffer to supper Sunday after next."

"Why wait so long?" asked my brother, who'd come in, too.

"I really don't know. It's your aunt's idea. She says that ought to give everybody enough time."

"Enough time for what?" I asked.

"Lucinda, I don't know. Your aunt said it had to do with Mr. Heffer and Mrs. Apley and not to pester her with idle questions. Adelina has a great deal on her mind these days."

She must be upset to use a rude word like *pester* to Mama. It made me think of Victor. "Is Victor Apley out in the kitchen with her, Mama?"

"No, he went off with your uncle. That was also her idea."

"Well, that's one way of getting rid of him."

Mama laughed and began to play with both hands again. "He does get on a person's nerves. All that energy should be put to good use. He crackles with it. I don't think he sleeps at all."

"I wish he'd go crackle somewhere else, Mama." Then I said, "I wonder if Willard is anything like his brother."

"His mother told me with pride that Willard is a great deal like his older brother—and possibly a bit more so."

I heaved a sigh, thinking of two Apley "cracklers" and patted Mama on the shoulder to comfort her. Then I headed for the kitchen. I doubted Aunt Adelina would order me out of it. After all, I'd gone with her into the wilderness and helped her pick and dig. And I was the one who had read the whole list of what was in the Tuscarora Tonic, not that I could begin to remember all the things, let alone their amounts. I knew that nobody else had read it because I'd heard her say she'd put it away along with her certificate of marriage. That certificate was always kept in the big old Westlake family Bible in the parlor.

I found her hunched over the kitchen table with paper,

pen, and ink in front of her, frowning while she scratched away on one of the sheets. Her reading spectacles had slipped down over the bridge of her nose.

As she raised her head to look at me, she pushed them back. "Oh, Lucinda, it's you. I heard someone just now at the back door. For a moment I thought it might be Victor."

"No, it was Henry Frederick and me. Mama says Victor has gone out to the Payday with Uncle Silas."

"Yes, that's right. What time is it?"

I didn't have to go out to the hall to look at the grandfather clock. I knew when Miss Hinkle let school out and how long it took for us to walk home when we didn't dally. "Four thirty."

"Good. I do believe that Gus Heffer must have put Victor to work already. That's really why I sent Victor out with Silas, so Silas could ask Heffer to give Victor a job, even if it may only be temporary. I didn't want to wait till the dinner party to get Victor working. When I heard someone at the back door, I was afraid Heffer had refused to hire him and Victor had come back."

I wasn't interested in Victor. The Bradshaw tonic was of more concern to me at the moment. I came around my aunt and daringly leaned over her shoulder to look at the papers spread out on the table. I asked, "Are you going to make the Tuscarora Tonic, Aunt Adelina, as our spring medicine?"

"No, Lucinda. I've studied it, and I simply can't do it as it's written down here. I am definitely going to have to make my own, as I told you out in the woods. Some parts of what I make will be like the recipe Bradshaw gave us. I've learned, though, that I can't follow it exactly ingredient by ingredient.

In the first place, some of the things don't grow out here. And in the second place, some of the others are far too expensive for my slender purse. I went to the stores in Denton and made inquiries about the tonic's herbs and roots. I found that a number of them aren't available in town, though I might order them from Portland. But when I saw the price lists for them, I nearly fainted. I bought a few of the cheaper ingredients, but I intend to rely very heavily on Oregon's wild native herbs and vegetation."

I sat down opposite her. "I want you to know that I will help you any way I can, Aunt Adelina."

"Thank you, Lucinda. I'll take you up on that offer. Eleanora and I will make the first batch of the tonic while you act as our helper in the kitchen when you aren't in school. I want you to promise me, though, that you will never reveal one single thing that goes into the tonic, not even to our own family or the Apleys. I pray that the day will come when the formula might be very valuable."

"I promise." Thunderation, this was exciting. I loved being sworn to secrecy.

"Eleanora and I will start to make our spring tonic tomorrow."

"What does Uncle Silas say about that?"

"Nothing. I've promised him that although the kitchen may smell a bit herbish and there may be pots on the back of the stove, he'll still have his meals on time. They may be simpler than usual, however, because I am working now."

I said, "I think Mama and Henry Frederick would help you, too."

"They can help. Your brother can dig more Oregon grape

roots, if I need them, and your mother can keep the house clean and play organ music to inspire Eleanora and me out in the kitchen. I lean to "Onward Christian Soldiers" these days. Now, Lucinda, be useful as well as ornamental. Pour me a cup of coffee from the pot while I get on with this formula."

After I'd done so, I said, "Why don't you call what you make the Tuscanook Tonic because it's got two Indian tribes mixed up with it now?"

"No, my dear." She paused with her pen in the air before she dipped it into the ink bottle. "I have already decided on a name. If this tonic should ever travel outside of the circle of the Howard, Westlake, and Apley families, it will be known as: Mrs. Westlake's Wonder-Working Elixir."

I could only exclaim in admiration, "Thunderation, that is a mouthful! I like the name. What's it going to do for people?"

"*Do?*" She looked sharply at me, and a little smile came over her face.

"Well, Aunt Adelina, if it works wonders, what kind of wonders will it work?"

She laughed outright now. "I think it will help stop just about every ailment that afflicts mankind and, in particular, womankind. I plan to put in powerful things to calm the nerves and brain. That's the reason I shall purchase mugwort, rue, pennyroyal, and valerian. I believe that most illnesses come out of the fevered mind. A strong, calm mind makes for a strong, healthy body."

"Your spring tonic ought to make us strong then."

"It might make Samsons of us all. Just about the only

thing it won't do is grow hair, I suspect. There won't be any lead in it, of course, and no sulphur either—not in my tonic! I have come to despise sulphur. Now, dear, please go give the lentils in the big blue-granite pot on the stove a stir and let me get on with my formula work."

What a queer, damp, earthy odor came from the kitchen that next afternoon when I got home after a hard day at school of not noticing or speaking to Caralee Lambertson, who shared a desk with me.

I found Mrs. Apley stirring two more big pots again and Aunt Adelina busy pounding what looked like brown twigs in a wooden bowl with a wooden mallet.

"This is a mortar and a pestle," she explained, as she dumped what was in the bowl into one of the big pots on the stove.

I sniffed the kitchen. It wasn't exactly a good odor or bad one either, but it sure was strong.

As my aunt picked up some very withered-looking, grayish plants, put them into the mortar, and began to pound the life out of them, I spotted some familiar-looking things on the kitchen table. Dandelion wine! The six bottles from the cellar. Four of them were empty and the fifth only half full.

I exclaimed, "That's the dandelion wine!"

"Of course it is, Lucinda. That's the solvent for my tonic. People are going to drink the tonic, you know. It has to be wet."

"But I thought you'd use water!"

"Water won't do, dear. We need body and flavor, which wine has but water doesn't."

"But, Aunt Adelina, I picked all those dandelions for the wine! It took me hours and hours and days and days."

"And you may yet pick thousands more, Lucinda." Aunt Adelina wasn't one bit sympathetic.

I plunked myself down and watched for a time, then said, "Won't a person who drinks that get drunk?" I'd seen drunks lying in the alleys behind Denton's saloons and thought it must be dreadful to get that way. And oh, how bad the drunken topers smelled.

My aunt said, "No, the alcohol evaporates away when the tonic is boiled."

That was good to hear.

Looking at Mrs. Apley made me think of Victor, so I asked, "Did Victor get a good job at the Payday?" I sincerely hoped that he had.

"Yes, indeed, Lucinda," said Mrs. Apley. "He and Mr. Heffer took highly to each other. My boy says he does about everything in there but serve beer and liquor and take a drink himself. My Victor knows where his head is. He won't ever be a toper. None of my boys will. They've been told the evils of demon rum from me."

I thought of Willard because she had spoken of her boys. "Did you write to Willard to come here, too?"

"No. I wrote him to hold his horses where he was and stay there till we got things more in hand here." All at once Mrs. Apley turned her head to look at my aunt. "Victor told me Gus Heffer's a plenty nice gent. He talked to Victor about that Kansas City widow, too. When Victor wanted to know why Heffer doted so much on a lady who didn't treat him too good, Mr. Heffer said it was because of her hair."

Hair? I shuddered by now at the very mention of that word. It would always make me think of Banker Lambertson.

"What about the lady's hair, Eleanora?" asked my aunt.

"Heffer told Victor that her hair was red as a new copper penny when he knew her as a girl. He told Victor that his heart almost stops beating when he catches sight of hair that color—even if it's on a dog."

Aunt Adelina asked over the sound of her pestle mashing more roots, "Weren't you a redhead once, Eleanora? Before you started to turn gray, that is?"

"Not so much a redhead as a strawberry blonde. I never did lean to the copper-penny color, though I like it." Mrs. Apley sighed as she rested the long wooden spoons for a moment.

My aunt told her, "You know, Eleanora, it might not be such a bad idea if your hair was the color of a new penny right now."

"Oh, missus, how would I do that? Get born all over again as a carrottop?"

"No, something far simpler than that. Henna is the answer. If you like, I'll send Lucinda to the store to buy a nickel's worth of henna. You can easily have the hair of your dreams and Mr. Heffer's dreams, too, by the night of our supper party."

Mrs. Apley was smiling as if she liked the idea. She seemed to have changed her mind about Mr. Heffer in a hurry. "Ah, I see what you mean, missus. If Gus Heffer dotes on red hair, then I'll get red hair to suit him."

"That's correct. But I would never suggest it if you didn't favor red hair too, Eleanora. After all, you have your pride.

Now don't forget, I want you to cook your very best dishes and bring them over here, so I can tell Mr. Heffer that you were the cook, not me."

I asked, "Will we be having fern pie again that night?"

"Fern pie?" answered Mrs. Apley, who was snorting in disgust. "No sirree. Victor found out yesterday what Mr. Heffer's favorite foods are—corned beef and cabbage and apple grunt with yellow cheese."

As I took the nickel Aunt Adelina gave me out of her sugar bowl, I thought of all that was going on in my life: being ruined, failing in the cosmetics business in two days, my busted friendship with Caralee, the spring elixir on our stove, and now Mrs. Apley's and Aunt Adelina's designs on unsuspecting Mr. Heffer. I couldn't help but wonder how things were going to turn out. If this was the sort of life most grown-ups led, no wonder they got gray hair.

I saw Mr. Heffer in the flesh, as I ran down to the pharmacy through a cloudburst. He was standing between the swinging doors of the Payday, chewing on his little moustache, staring out into the sheets of gray rain. What a sad and mournful expression he had on his face. It looked to me as if he'd lost his last friend on earth. Maybe he was thinking of the widow in Kansas City.

Because I felt sorry for him and because he couldn't recognize me under my big sou'wester hat, I cried out to him as I passed, "Buck up, Mr. Heffer. Love is on its winging way to you." That was something I'd read in a book Caralee had loaned me. He couldn't say now that he hadn't been warned.

And then on I went, after he'd looked goggle-eyed at me and ducked back between the swinging doors. That would give him something to think about and perhaps put him in the right frame of mind to admire Mrs. Apley when he got to know her at the supper.

After I got back to my aunt's kitchen with the henna powder in a brown-paper enevlope, I told Aunt Adelina and Mrs. Apley what I'd said. Mrs. Apley beamed while my aunt only nodded. "Well, that was mighty sassy and bold of you, Lucinda. But you're right in one thing—he's not likely to forget what you said."

A little bit later, before the last of the dandelion wine got poured into the pots and while Mrs. Apley had her back turned to us, I whispered, "Aunt Adelina, what does Mr. Whitlow have to say about Mr. Heffer and her?" I pointed to Mrs. Apley.

"He approves, Lucinda. He is very much aware that we are plotting a good deed. And he approves of my other reasons for asking Gus Heffer to supper."

"What are they?" I whispered again.

"My secrets, Lucinda. That's what they are."

Secrets? Two of them—or maybe more. I waited for her to swear me to secrecy and tell me, but she didn't say another word.

The next afternoon I knew the minute I came in the front door that something was wrong. In spite of the rain all of the downstairs windows were wide open and cold air was blowing through the house. Mama wasn't anywhere to be seen, though Uncle Silas was. He was sitting in the parlor reading from the *Oregonian* and looking very down at the mouth.

I asked, "Did you go to see Mr. Lamberston again today?" I supposed that was why he had the sour look on his face.

"No, I didn't go near Lambertson or the bank. I know that would be about as useful as pouring sand down a rathole. It's your aunt, Lucinda."

"Is she sick?"

"You might say that in a way she is."

"Is she upstairs in bed? If she is, she's going to get pneumonia with all the windows open." Right at that moment a lace curtain was blowing into the parlor, across the top of the cottage organ.

"The ladies are all out in the kitchen. Go join them, Lucinda. Leave me, a mere man, out here in peace."

So that's where I went without even taking off my sou'wester hat. There they were—Aunt Adelina, Mama, and Mrs. Apley. They all appeared to me to be very low in spirits, as they sat staring at the six bottles that had been full of clear, golden dandelion wine and were now full of something dark and murky brown.

I asked, "What's the matter?"

The big pots were off the stove. The mortar was gone and the pestle, too, and so were the jars and packets of herbs and roots. It wasn't at all unusual for my aunt's kitchen to be neat, but now it looked positively empty.

The only bright item in it was Mrs. Apley—not her face, which was melancholy, but her bright, copper-red hair. I gaped at it. It blazed away like a bonfire in the still kitchen.

"Lucinda," Aunt Adelina said, as she held out a clean teaspoon from the table where there were other teaspoons lined up. "Please taste our elixir and tell me truthfully what you think of it."

I took the spoon, poured out a bit from the bottle nearest me, put it to my tongue, and then swallowed.

I gagged. It was bitter, so bitter that I felt my mouth puckering and my jaws starting to ache.

"You see, missus, her eyes are bugging out, too," said Mrs. Apley sadly. "She didn't have a conniption fit like my Zenobia, but she doesn't like it either."

"Yes, I can see that for myself, Eleanora."

"I couldn't keep much of that stuff down in my stomach," I told my aunt, once I could speak again. "Thunderation, that's a mouthful!" I longed to go to the backyard pump, where they couldn't see me, and rinse out my mouth with water. How I hoped we weren't going to have to take *this* everyday as our spring tonic.

Aunt Adelina leaned her head into her hand, supporting herself by one elbow, and said, "When it comes to its taste, I am forced to admit that this elixir is a failure. Or at least this version of it is a failure."

Mrs. Apley said, "You should have put the wine into the tonic straight from the wine bottle. But it's all gone anyhow, ain't it?"

I put in, "Yes, and I'm afraid there aren't any dandelions in bloom now."

"Dandelion wine isn't the answer in any event," said Aunt Adelina. "And even if we hadn't boiled the wine, the elixir would taste the same—frightful. That wine cannot be the solvent I am looking for." She looked up at me. "Lucinda, I think we've let enough breeze into this house to get rid of all of the odor of the elixir by now. Would you please go around and shut the parlor and hall windows while I close up in here?"

Aunt Adelina went to stand sadly at the window that looked out onto the hen house and pigsty. She was murmuring as she brushed the damp white-muslin curtains out of the way to get hold of the window. "Into every life a little rain must fall. Let that be a lesson to all of us." Her voice grew stronger. "But I am not licked yet—or my name isn't Adelina Pinkerton Westlake! I have hope."

I saw how Mama stared at her and Mrs. Apley, too. They'd both lifted their heads to look at her.

Aunt Adelina looked like a statue at that moment, a quite small one to be sure, but a statue of somebody who was bold as a lion. I tried to think of some lady I'd read about who was a bold and brave fighter and deserving of a statue. There were lots of statues of men, generals and admirals and so on, but none of brave ladies.

And then all at once I thought of one. The lady knight in the shining armor—Joan of Arc!

CHAPTER VI

"They Were Something of a Surprise to Me, Too."

Another failure! Thunderation, this was terrible. The date Uncle Silas had to pay Mr. Bradshaw's debt at the bank was coming closer minute by minute. I couldn't help but think about the man who'd left town and given my uncle only forty-eight dollars and the formula for the tonic. No, I hadn't ever taken to Bradshaw. He grinned a great deal, showing a mouthful of big teeth, but that grin could vanish just as fast as it could show up. Most of his lower face was teeth and ginger-colored whiskers, and the upper part was lots of curling, gingery-brown hair. I hadn't wished Barlow Bradshaw well when we'd failed in our cosmetic business, and now that we'd failed again by using his tonic recipe, I wished him even less well. I'd have liked to roll Mr. Bradshaw and Banker Lambertson together in a great big snow-ball and shove it down a steep hill.

And there was somebody else I wasn't so happy with either, though I wasn't sure I should call him a man. I was thinking of Mr. Whitlow!

He'd let my aunt believe she was doing the right thing two times. I'd even heard the second banging sound, the one in Mrs. Apley's kitchen. It didn't seem to me that he was so terribly trustworthy either. After all, he was supposed to have lived a dismaying life on this planet—one so dismaying Mama wouldn't even talk about it. This worried me. I figured I'd better take up the subject of Mr. Whitlow again with Mama, who had had more experience with Aunt Adelina's spirits than I.

So after supper, while Henry Frederick and Aunt Adelina were hauling the tonic made from our dandelion wine out to the shed next to the pigsty, I cornered Mama in the parlor. She was playing a soft waltz to comfort Uncle Silas as I whispered to her, "Mama, Aunt Adelina claims that Mr. Whitlow said she should make the cosmetics and the tonic, but they didn't work out. Has she said anything to you about his doing that?"

She shook her head and whispered over the waltz, "No, Lucinda, but I took it on myself to ask her after Mrs. Apley went home. Your aunt said that the spirits are inclined more often than not to give messages about the final result of some work a person has in mind. They don't take much account of the failures along the way. She has hope it will all come right in the end."

I complained, "That's all right, I suppose, but failing twice is pretty hard on people. I'll bet it's easier to be a spirit and just float around giving advice than to be a person working toward a final result."

"What're you two whispering about? Plotting something against somebody?" Uncle Silas called out. He was still in a bad mood, and no wonder. When I left Mama's side, he asked me, "What's Adelina doing with that God-awful, smelly stuff she made?"

"Henry Frederick's going to mix it in with the pig food. Aunt Adelina says it's a tonic and ought to be healthful, even if it doesn't taste too good."

He muttered, "I hope she knows what she's doing to the hogs. I don't want the pork to taste like that stuff smells." And he went back to his book of essays, glaring at the page.

The week afterward, Aunt Adelina and I went back to the woods again to get more ferns for fern pie and more roots and herbs. She had the herbs drying all over the kitchen for days. Oregon's damp climate was bad for herb gathering, she told me.

I guessed that she was going to try the tonic again, and she was fiddling with more papers on the kitchen table whenever I came home from school, where I was still ignoring Caralee and having her ignore me.

Losing Caralee as a friend threw me more into the company of my brother. But all he could talk about was Victor Apley and the Apley pigs and our pigs. It seemed to me that whenever he wasn't in school and Victor not working at the Payday Saloon, they were together at either our sty or at the Apley sty.

I told Henry Frederick near the end of that week, "You and Victor are sure taken with pigs these days, aren't you?"

"They're interesting, Lucinda, and so is Victor, lots more interesting than I thought he was at first. And the hogs dote on Aunt Adelina's tonic. All Victor and I have to do is pour it on the slop and swill, and they go crazy gobbling it up."

"Ugh!" I made a face, feeling glad that feeding the hens and gathering the eggs were my chore instead of slopping the pigs.

"The little pigs are growing faster than ever these days. They're really putting on the lard and getting frisky and— other things, too." Henry Frederick told me, as he leaped over a small puddle not worth wading through.

I said, "Well, I'm glad to hear that something's getting the benefit of all those dandelion heads." Then I walked faster to outdistance him and his talk of hogs and Victor Apley.

When I got home I went out to my aunt in the kitchen. "Victor says our pigs are eating their heads off these days. It seems they dote on the dandelion-wine tonic," I said.

My aunt was so busy with the papers in front of her on the kitchen table that she didn't even look up. But she said, "I'm surely glad to hear that. Lord knows even the pigs aren't eating like they once did around here. I'm happy that they like fern pie, boiled dried vegetables, and bread. I want them to be plump when slaughtering time comes this fall and I fix salt pork, so we'll have several well-filled barrels to get us through what might be a very slim winter." Now she did look up at me. "Would you like to go to Portland with me tomorrow morning, Lucinda? I have some errands there."

"Sure, I would." I'd gone to Portland on the old stagecoach a couple of times but not on the train. It had only just come through Denton on its way down to Roseburg, which was the end of the line so far. The train went at the almost frightening speed of forty miles an hour. A person could go up to Portland and do some errands and be back in Denton by dark.

"What errands do you have, Aunt Adelina?"

"Some secret ones—secret from your Uncle Silas, that is."

"You can tell me. I promise not to tell anybody."

"I know you won't, Lucinda, because I'm not going to say what they are. Let that be a lesson to you. To keep a secret, don't tell anybody at all."

"But you'll have to give him a reason for going."

She asked me quietly, "Does he give me a reason for going over to the Payday Saloon so often?"

"No, but I thought you'd changed your mind about Mr. Heffer?"

"In a way I have, but I still do not truly approve of his line of business. Your Uncle Silas plans to go fishing tomorrow morning. You and I will leave for the depot as soon as he's headed for the Willamette River."

"Does Mama know? Did you tell Henry Frederick?"

"She knows. He has not been told and will not be told. Mrs. Apley, though, gives her blessing as well as some sorely needed cash."

Because Uncle Silas went fishing at daybreak, we had a full hour to get ready to board the Portland-bound train. Walking together under her big umbrella, Aunt Adelina and I got to the depot ten minutes early by her lapel watch and boarded the waiting train. I'd seen the red-and-gold cars and black locomotive pass through Denton many a time, but what a thrill it was to climb up the metal steps and sit down on the velvet seats. The train jerked and jolted starting out for Portland, but then it soon settled down to its terrific speed that made the scenery whiz by outside the windows.

"Lucinda, don't stare too hard at what we're passing," my aunt warned me. "It could make you dizzy. Railroad men have gone mad because of speed. A craving for speed destroys sinew, brain, bone, and muscle. But, on the other hand, speed will get us to Portland and back in one day, so Silas won't have more to be angry about. We'll eat the lunch I've brought with us in the Portland depot on the way back."

Portland, which lay on the west bank of the Willamette, not far from the great Columbia River, was Oregon's biggest city. I didn't know how many people lived there, but there seemed to be lots more than in Denton. Every time I'd come up by stagecoach before I'd seen more buildings. The town was always full of the noise of sawmills cutting timber and hammers nailing buildings together. And it wasn't any less noisy this time. Portland was being built faster than ever now because parts of it had burned down the year before.

The houses were mostly of wood because Oregon had so much timber, but I noticed that some newer, mighty handsome business offices were made of bricks, cast iron, and stone. The post office, for one, was so big and tall that it made me gasp. Yes, Portland was a busy and important city with dozens and dozens of stores and shops.

I'd expected Aunt Adelina to head straight for Portland's pharmacies once we'd left the First Street depot, but she didn't. She went past three of them and stopped finally in front of a little shop not too far from the depot. It had a queer sign with three balls hanging over the door.

"Lucinda, you stay outside," she ordered me. "This errand should not take me very long."

But it did. A half gallon of rain must have run off the umbrella I was holding before she came out. Looking plenty angry, she said to me, "All that miserable man would give me was twenty dollars, and he said he was being generous at that."

"What did he give you twenty dollars for?"

"For my lapel watch. I just pawned it. This is a pawnshop. Come on, let's go to the large pharmacy down on Second Street. I'll have my list filled there." She grabbed the umbrella from me and started out at a pace that made me half run to keep up with her. She was tiny, but she was surely a fast walker.

"What's a pawnshop?" I had never heard of anything called a pawn, outside of a chess piece.

"It is a place of despair. People who need cash surrender their beloved treasures to pawnbrokers for a fraction of their value, and the pawnbrokers keep them for thirty or sixty or ninety days. If the person who pawns the treasure doesn't return to buy it back in time, the pawnbroker sells it at a profit to somebody else."

That was bad to hear. I said, "That's another grown-up fact, huh?"

"That's correct. Whatever you do, don't tell Silas about the pawnshop. I plan to get the watch back, but right now I'll use the twenty dollars for herbs and roots."

I asked, "What if he asks why you don't wear the watch?"

She sighed. "If he does, I'll tell him the minute hand is stuck and it needs repairing, or something like that."

The pharmacy on Second Street was busy, but the clerks got right to work on Aunt Adelina's list, weighing on scales things they took from little wooden drawers on a wall and from shiny cream-colored jars, and then putting them into little bags and envelopes. While Aunt Adelina watched the scales, I wandered over to the front window to admire the great big bottles of blue- and red-liquid medicine standing among some other smaller bottles.

A clerk came over to me after a while and asked, "Can I do something for you, little girl?"

I told him, "I'm not a little girl. I'm with her." I pointed to my aunt. Then I asked, "What does the blue tonic do and what does the red one do? Is the red one peppermint flavored?"

He laughed and told me, "No, they don't do a single thing. They just stand around and look ornamental, little girl. They're only colored water and just for show."

I thought this seemed dishonest but didn't get to tell him because he left me to go wait on a real customer.

I watched Aunt Adelina pay out twenty-four dollars for the things she'd bought, which couldn't weigh more than a pound and a couple of ounces. Herbs and roots cost plenty! Then, after she put her purchases in the cloth bag she was carrying, we went out.

We walked down Second Street until we turned onto Jefferson Street. There she stopped in front of another pharmacy, a little one, and handed me the bag. "Stay out here. Keep this out of the rain, please. This will take only a minute. Then we'll go to the depot and eat our lunch."

This time she was right. She was in and out of there in only about three minutes, snapping her little, black-beaded reticule shut as she came down the steps.

"What did you buy here, Aunt Adelina?"

"Nothing, Lucinda." She was smiling.

But why if she hadn't bought anything was she shutting her reticule? Maybe she'd bought something small, just one little piece of root or a tiny packet of something. Well, I knew two of her secrets by watching her, but not the third one: what she'd bought in this little pharmacy.

We were in luck. We got home a half hour before Uncle Silas came in with a salmon and some bass he'd caught. My aunt and I were out of our good clothing, the herbs and roots had been put away in the big pantry, and we were all sitting in the parlor while Mama played a Brahms lullaby on the cottage organ.

Uncle Silas seemed to be in a better mood than I'd seen him in for days. He told us, "Gus Heffer was out fishing with me. He says he's sure looking forward to a home-cooked supper tomorrow night over here."

"Did you put in a good word for Eleanora?" Aunt Adelina asked him.

"I mentioned to him that she'd be here with her little girls."

"That's fine, Silas. He won't be surprised then."

Now that was a supper I'll never forget! It was almost as unusual as New Year's Eve.

Mrs. Apley came over in midafternoon with covered dishes of food, which Aunt Adelina put into the warming oven while Mama and I set the table. Mrs. Apley came back at seven thirty, dressed up more elegantly than I'd ever seen her in a gown of serpent-green taffeta with jet buttons and black lace at the cuffs and neckline. Zenobia and Yolanda were scrubbed pink and wearing white-muslin dresses with violet-satin sashes. Victor was there, too, off work, I supposed, and looking very splendid in a gray suit with black-and-brown checks, a red-silk tie, and brown vest.

We Howards and Westlakes, who wore our New Year's Eve clothes, were put in the shade by the Apleys and even more in the shade by Mr. Heffer, who came at seven forty-five. He wore a dove-gray frock coat and trousers and a vest of silver-and-rose brocade. The vest buttons, which shone in the parlor lamplight, were of solid gold, I was sure.

Mr. Heffer sat down with us in the parlor while Aunt Adelina got the food on the table, and it seemed to me that Mr. Heffer behaved quite peculiarly. I watched him carefully and saw how he kept glancing again and again at Victor, puffing out his cheeks and making his moustache rise and fall. Then he'd look away as if he was angry about something. I also took notice that he didn't once speak to Victor, who after all was his employee, and he didn't have anything but yes or no to say to Mrs. Apley when she tried to talk to him. He acted positively peeved at all of them.

Mama and Uncle Silas were the ones he talked to—not to the Apleys, not even to the girls, and not to me and Henry Frederick. Mostly he carried on a conversation with Mama while she embroidered. His eyes would flick right past the Apleys to rest on Mama's face.

By the time we'd all been called into the dining room, I was wondering what was wrong with Mr. Heffer. Something surely was, but I couldn't pin down what it was.

To make things go easier, I whispered to Mr. Heffer, who was seated next to me and just across from Mrs. Apley so he could admire her, "That's corned beef and cabbage in the tureen Uncle Silas is taking the lid off of now. It's Mrs. Apley's favorite dish. She cooked it for us tonight—not Aunt Adelina."

As he tucked his big white napkin into his collar, he said sharply with his eyes fixed on his empty plate, not on Mrs. Apley, "Do tell? I thought maybe the cook tonight was the mighty pretty dark-headed lady on the other side of you."

"Oh, she's my mother." I saw to my horror that he was leaning back in his chair peering past me at Mama. Thunderation, was he taken with Mama? Come to think of it, that's just how he acted in the parlor. Well, I had to try to put a stop to that right now in order to help Mrs. Apley. I swallowed hard, gathered all my courage, and whispered to him, "Mr. Heffer, my mother is a terrible cook, so Aunt Adelina does all of the cooking in this house. Mama's afraid that the man she's secretly engaged to down in California— the one she writes to three times a week—won't like the way she burns and scorches everything. She boils roasts of beef and pork chops."

I saw him shake his head. "Somehow, she don't look the type to do that sort of thing."

I glanced at Mama and then at everybody else. They weren't paying any heed to me, so I whispered, "Oh, but she does. That's because she's always got her nose in a book of poetry or is playing the cottage organ. She doesn't give a hoot for housekeeping."

"Oh, a weak sister, huh? Is she given to the vapors, too?"

I nodded as I got my plate of food from Uncle Silas. "You might say that, Mr. Heffer. Now you take Mrs. Apley—she's strong as an ox, and she hardly ever reads at all."

He was finally looking at her. Mrs. Apley was especially handsome at that moment, too. She was smiling at Uncle Silas, who'd just given her a plate. That serpent-green color and the black lace certainly showed off her new hair color.

I said to Heffer, "Hasn't she got the prettiest hair, though? It's just the color of a new copper penny."

He mumbled something rather dismaying. "I doubt that it's real, though."

Nervously I rattled on about her hair. "Well, I don't know for sure about the color, but the hair is real. She doesn't pin on any hairpieces, ever. She's got lots and lots of hair that's all her own. It's so long she can sit on it when she lets it down."

Heffer was chewing on a piece of corned beef now, so he didn't say anything for a bit. Then he wiped off his moustache and told me, "Well, I got to admit this is mighty good food. She's a dandy little cook, all right. I have to hand that to her."

Encouraged, I asked, "Aren't her little girls pretty, though?"

"Ahem." That was a coughing sound I recognized. It had come from Aunt Adelina. When I looked at her across the way, I caught her eyes on me, and I knew what they were telling me. She didn't want me to take up all of Mr. Heffer's time with my chatter.

"Yep, them girls are cunning little dickenses. You say they haven't got a papa now?" That was the right sort of thing for him to say, all right.

"Oh, no, sir, they haven't got any father." So I told him how Mr. Apley had gone to his reward.

Heffer nodded, then said, "That's a sad story, and my heart goes out to the little widow woman, but her family don't appear to me to have much good sense."

"What do you mean, Mr. Heffer?"

After a big bite of slippery cabbage, he said, "That galoot of a Victor Apley is supposed to be working in my saloon this very minute, sweeping out the back room and storeroom. He knows he should be at work, and I know it. If that's so, what is he doing here at your aunt's dinner table? I sure don't like that kind of behavior from my hired help."

This was dreadful! I gawked at Victor, who acted as if he didn't have a care in the world but shoving his supper in his mouth. I decided he had to be crazy to be here eating when he should have been at work. Because I was so embarrassed and flustered by what he was doing to his mother, I stopped talking and kept my eyes on my plate while I finished my own corned beef and cabbage. Dang that silly Victor. He could be spoiling everything.

Aunt Adelina tried to make conversation at the table after I'd stopped chatting with Mr. Heffer. Nobody seemed inclined to talk, though. The most anybody would say was a word here and there about how good the food tasted and to ask for second helpings out of the tureen.

Finally the time came for the apple grunt, which was sliced baked apples in piecrust with cream poured over the top. Yellow cheese was served on the side since Mr. Heffer liked cheese with his apple grunt. I said, while I started in on mine, "Mr. Heffer, folks say this is called apple grunt because when you eat it, you always grunt for more."

By saying the word *grunt* I unfortunately opened the door for Henry Frederick to get around to the subject of pigs. He asked, "Hey, Mr. Heffer, do you like hogs? Victor and I are raising pigs, and they're doing just fine these days."

Before Mr. Heffer could say if he did or didn't like pigs, Victor lifted his head from his apple grunt and snapped at my brother. "I'm not raising pigs with you. Pigs ain't in my line of work, little boy."

"But, Victor, you help me slop them all the time," answered my brother.

I gasped. Victor Apley must have really and truly lost his mind to say that.

"Now you went and did it," cried Mrs. Apley. "You went and spoiled the big surprise I was planning to give us all with the coffee tonight. This big handsome boy ain't what you all think he is!"

"I think I know what he is," Mr. Heffer said, in a voice like a block of ice. "I can't go any longer without speaking my piece! He is my one-time employee Victor Apley. He is a work shirker. That's what he is. He should be hit with a baking-powder biscuit. I'm a guest in this house, and I don't want to cause trouble, but, Victor Apley, you ain't working for me anymore. Do you hear me?"

To my horror, Victor let out a loud, ringing laugh.

Mrs. Apley cried out, "Oh, Mr. Heffer, you don't get my meaning. This ain't Victor at all. This is his little brother Willard. Victor's at work where he ought to be."

Willard? Everybody was gaping at the young man who was a dead ringer for Victor. Twins. They had to be twins!

"Yes, sirree, my boys are twins, like two peas in the same

pod. Victor's five minutes older than Willard. They've always been a big surprise to a lot of folks. They were something of a surprise to me, too, because when they came along I wasn't expecting two babies."

"Twins, huh?" came from Mr. Heffer, who put down his spoon. "Well, young man, if you aren't my employee, may I ask where you've been holed up all this time?"

Willard's voice was just like his brother's. "Up in Idaho Territory working in a general store. I came down here to visit Ma before I start looking for work in Oregon. Things are slow up in Idaho Territory now."

"Hmm," was all that Heffer said, as he went on with his dessert.

Nobody paid Mr. Heffer any more heed, because they were so busy asking Willard questions about Idaho Territory.

After supper, we sat around the table for a time until Zenobia yawned and Mrs. Apley said, "It appears to me that I ought to see these younguns home and into bed. They've got to go to school tomorrow." She smiled at Mr. Heffer. "It was a pleasure to make your acquaintance, Mr. Heffer, and I think it's fine of you to give my Victor a job. You have the nicest, brightest-yellow whiskey saloon in all of Denton."

"Thank you, Mrs. Apley." He was smiling at her. Since he'd learned about Victor still being at work, he'd mellowed.

She said softly, "My name's Eleanora, Mr. Heffer."

He nodded as he took the cigar Uncle Silas passed down the table to him. Of course, he didn't smoke it there; that would come later. Gentlemen smoked but not at the table with ladies.

Mr. Heffer spoke to Zenobia this time. "What's your name, little bright eyes?"

She said, yawning again and with her eyes half closed, "It's Zenobia Zuleika Apley."

"And what's your sister's name?"

Yolanda replied, "I'm Yolanda Yvonne Apley."

Mr. Heffer looked at Mrs. Apley. "Well, now, that is something, isn't it? You've got a Z.Z. and a Y.Y., huh?"

"Yes, it was my late husband's idea. He was Abner Albert Apley. Victor is Victor Vernon. Willard is Willard Wilbur."

"That's me, all right," put in Willard.

Heffer smiled and said, "The names start at the wrong end of the alphabet. But why not start there instead of at the front? Well, Zenobia Zuleika and Yolanda Yvonne, I spotted a circus poster the other day on the wall of a store. There's a circus coming to Denton next week. How would you like the idea of my taking the two of you and your ma to see it?"

I saw how the girls' eyes opened wide all at once, but they didn't answer him. Instead Mrs. Apley said, "Oh, Mr. Heffer, they'd just love that!"

Then she got up out of her chair and yanked Zenobia out of hers. Willard went home with them too as Uncle Silas and Mr. Heffer went into the parlor. Mama and I cleaned the table off together, while Henry Frederick ran out with a lantern to see his beloved hogs. Aunt Adelina went into the parlor with the two men. After a bit I smelled cigar smoke, something she hated, and I was sure she'd be right out, but she didn't come. Uncle Silas was the one who appeared, saying, as he passed Mama and me, "I'm going to fetch my last bottle of port wine. How about you getting out the tray and two glasses, Lucinda?"

"Yes, sir." Getting up on a stool to reach the top cupboard, I brought down the little cut-glass glasses, rinsed off the dust, wiped them, and put them on the tray.

He must have had trouble finding the bottle he wanted because I was back in the parlor before he was.

And what did I see but my aunt standing beside Mr. Heffer, who was staring solemnly into her face, nodding and nodding, while she talked to him. And then she did a most remarkable thing, something I had never seen a lady do before: she put out her right hand to him. He took it, *shaking hands with her*, a lady! Thunderation!

Then she turned her head to look at me. "Oh, Lucinda, fine. Put the tray and glasses down there. Your uncle will pour the wine." She inclined her head to Mr. Heffer and went out before I could even get the tray down.

Mr. Heffer didn't pay any more attention to me, so out I went to find Aunt Adelina removing the damask tablecloth Zenobia had spilled apple grunt on.

"Do you think the supper was a success?" I asked her.

"Yes, Lucinda, I do. It was a whopper of a success."

"Why were you shaking hands with Mr. Heffer just now?"

"I wasn't. He said he wanted me to see how rough his hands were and was asking if I thought he could use a jar of my Persian Pool Hand Soother."

Before I could say anything further she went out of the dining room to the back porch to soak the tablecloth in the filled laundry tub. The way she'd acted when I asked her that question made me decide not to ask it again.

My, but the night had been full of surprises—and they hadn't all been Willard Apley either! I wished I could tell Caralee Lambertson about them, but we still weren't on speaking terms.

That next afternoon when I came home from school, I got another surprise. I found Mrs. Apley and my aunt out in the kitchen, but before I could ask Mrs. Apley if she'd liked Mr. Heffer as much as I thought she had, there was a rap at the kitchen door.

A head wearing a sou'wester filled the doorway; then a man's voice called, "Open up, Mrs. Westlake, hurry up. This is heavy."

I went to the door. I knew Victor's voice, or was this Willard?

A man carrying a wooden keg on his shoulder pushed past me and set the keg down on the kitchen floor.

"Are you my Victor or are you my Willard?" asked Mrs. Apley.

"Victor, Ma. This is grain alcohol from the Payday Saloon. It's for Mrs. Westlake to use in her next try at a tonic. Gus Heffer told me to get right on back to his saloon after you give me that jar of hand soother he ordered last night, Mrs. Westlake."

My aunt stared at the keg, and then she said, "How wonderful. Silas has changed his mind about my going into business."

Mrs. Apley asked, "Do you mean to say, missus, that your husband sent over this keg?"

"Well, of course, Eleanora. Mr. Heffer must have made

him see the light last night when they had the port wine and cigars in the parlor." My aunt pointed to me. "Lucinda, please go up to my bedroom and fetch a jar of hand cream from the top drawer of my bureau."

I ran upstairs and down and gave the cream to Victor, who stuffed it into his mackintosh pocket and went out.

"Now, Eleanora and Lucinda, I must speak to you." Aunt Adelina went to stand in front of her stove with her arms folded over her chest. "We must not embarrass Silas by telling how much we appreciate his getting Mr. Heffer to send over the solvent for my next tonic. Silas has done another good deed. He likes to have his good deeds go unsung, so please don't mention this latest one to him."

I asked, "You mean the way he helped Barlow Bradshaw?"

"Exactly, Lucinda. In this case Silas is striving to make up for his refusal to help me make the tonic to begin with. He must somehow have made a gentleman's agreement with Mr. Heffer to buy this alcohol on credit. I think Silas now has faith in me. Let's swear never to make him sad by reminding him of his earlier behavior and actions. He has repented."

"Oh, I swear," came from Mrs. Apley.

I said, "I swear, too, Aunt Adelina, but I think it's rather peculiar."

At that moment there was a click from what seemed to be the coffee cup next to me—just as if somebody had flicked it with a fingernail.

It was he! I knew it. Had Aunt Adelina heard him, too? I stared at her and saw that she had begun to smile. Thunderation!

CHAPTER VII

An Extremely Silent Partner

Of course I expected my aunt and Mrs. Apley to get busy right away on the second batch of tonic, and they did. That Tuesday afternoon when my brother and I came up onto the back porch we found a *Women at Work* sign, so around to the front we went.

Henry Frederick and I both sniffed the air in the hallway, and I agreed with him when he said, "Hey, it smells lots better than the first time."

True. This tonic had a sort of grassy, woodsy smell, and I thought of the words Uncle Silas had once used, *weeds from the wilderness.* That was it—a sort of wilderness odor.

I went to the kitchen, and Henry Frederick went out to the pigs. Mama was stirring pots along with Mrs. Apley, while Aunt Adelina pounded things in her wooden bowl and looked at some sheets of paper in front of her.

I said, "It smells good. What color is it going to be?"

"We won't know," said my aunt, "until we put the solvent in at the very last moment."

I told her, "I'll bet I know what your solvent is going to be for this batch." I pointed to the wooden keg beside the stove. "Aunt Adelina, you aren't going to boil it, are you?"

"No, not this time."

"But, that's *alcohol*, Aunt Adelina!"

"So it is, Lucinda."

"But people who take the tonic might get drunk on it!"

She gave me a sharp look, while Mrs. Apley chuckled. "No, they won't. They'll take a tablespoonful at a time, that's all. If someone foolishly tries more than a half cup, I can guarantee you that they will get sick and lose whatever they drank."

"Oh." I was glad to hear this. I leaned against the closed kitchen door and asked, "Where's Uncle Silas?"

"Out trying to sell the carriage. Banker Lambertson might buy it."

I made a face. Lambertson again? I still wasn't speaking to Caralee at school, and she was ignoring me, though sharing the same desk made it hard. Because she was left-handed and I was right-handed, her elbow kept bumping into my side when she reached for a book in the drawer under the desk. Oh, well, I didn't care who Uncle Silas sold the carriage to as long as he could get a buyer. There were few things in life more useless than a carriage without a horse to pull it.

Mrs. Apley said, "I hear tell that awful la grippe sickness has come down to Denton from Portland."

"That's right," I said. "One of the third-grade kids is out of school because he caught it. His whole family is down with it, or so Miss Hinkle says."

Aunt Adelina said, "Eleanora, I hope to have this tonic ready tomorrow afternoon so we can start taking it, no matter how it might taste. I believe it will preserve us all from la grippe and head colds."

"I sure hope so, missus."

"Amen to that," came from Mama.

When I got home the next afternoon I found the kitchen more full of folks than I'd ever seen it—all of the Apleys, Mama, and my aunt—and the top of the kitchen table was loaded with filled and corked bottles.

What was in them was a rather nice shade of green, a Brewster green, the same color that was on the trim of the horse carriage. The whole kitchen smelled of ferns and deep places in the woods.

"Try it, Lucinda, taste it." I could hear the triumph in Aunt Adelina's voice, as she handed me the one open bottle along with a teaspoon.

I tasted it.

It slid nicely over my tongue and down my throat. It wasn't bitter, and it wasn't sweet. I decided that it had a cool licorice taste, which I doted on. "You did it this time, Aunt Adelina!" I even smacked my lips. "It's not tasty enough to want much of, but at the same time you don't feel you're punishing yourself when you take it."

"Good, that's what I wanted to hear."

"Yep, Mrs. Westlake, you got your verdict out of the

mouths of babes and children," exclaimed Victor—or was it Willard?

"I am *not* a child!"

But nobody heard me. They were all talking at once, even Zenobia and Yolanda.

Finally one of the twins said, "Silence, everyone! I'm Victor. That's Willard. My brother and I made a decision even before we tasted this second tonic. We decided that if it was good, we would try to sell it. We'll get hold of some bottles, load up carpetbags with them, and head out to get orders for Mrs. Westlake's elixir."

Willard said, "Victor's tired of working in a saloon. He was cut out for better things, and so am I."

"You two lads were indeed," agreed their mother.

"But the tonic hasn't been tried out yet," said Mama.

"No, but the earlier one has," said Victor. "It's been tried for some time."

I put in angrily because he was so smart-acting, "Nobody ever took it, Victor Apley!"

"Nobody human did." Victor lifted a long bony finger to silence me. "But you are forgetting the pigs. The pigs are doing magnificently on it. What is happening to the pigs is—"

Willard broke in on his brother. "I've written up some testimonials from citizens of Denton about the benefits of Mrs. Westlake's Wonder-Working Elixir. Hear this one." He took a piece of paper from his vest pocket and read aloud, "'I hereby swear that this tonic has whetted my appetite and lifted my spirits greatly in only one week's time.' It's signed 'Mrs. Denton Hogg and family.' Here's the other one. 'I wish to state that I have never found a tonic to do so much for my state of health in so short a time as Mrs. Westlake's Wonder-Working Elixir,' signed 'Mr. Apley Bohr and family.'"

I said, "Thunderation," and sat down at the table next to Mama, who was already down.

Mama told Williard, "But those are pigs, and it isn't the same tonic!"

He asked Aunt Adelina, "Mrs. Westlake, doesn't tonic number one have just about the same things in it as number two?"

"Well, not exactly, Victor. There are some added and changed ingredients."

"But will number two harm anybody who takes it?"

"No, it certainly will not." I saw how she was shaking her head. "I guarantee that it won't. It is a helpful but perfectly harmless herbal elixir."

"That's all me and Willard need to know. I'll go scour around town for some sample bottles the right size, while Willard makes up a label to put on them."

"A label?" My aunt sounded surprised. "I hadn't thought of that."

"Well, me and Willard have. We even know what we want to be on the label."

I guessed what they had in mind. "All right, what kind of Indian are you thinking of?" I asked.

Willard laughed. "No Indian at all. What I aim to do is sketch a picture of Mrs. Westlake's face and put *it* on the label."

"*No!*" wailed Mama.

As for me, I was too stunned to let out a peep. I knew

why Mama had cried out. Respectable ladies' names and faces were not printed or written in public places. I'd never heard of a Denton lady who had her name in a shopwindow —let alone on a bottle label. What an idea!

There was such a silence in the kitchen that even Zenobia quit tugging at her mother's apron and stared up at her, wondering what had suddenly gone wrong.

"Well, Mrs. Westlake, it's your tonic, you know," said Victor.

"It's your tonic, and it's your face," added Willard.

"Ah, so they are—both of them." She sighed deeply, then said, "I confess I'd hoped that this second tonic would be good enough to be sold outside of Denton. I need money badly. That's no secret to anyone. Yes, I know that if you are to try to sell the tonic, there has to be a label on the bottles, and the tonic must have a name. But in my wildest dreams and hopes I never conceived of the idea of having *my* face on the label. The idea is enough to take a lady's breath away!"

Victor said, "Mrs. Westlake, seeing a lady's face on a label would give lady customers confidence in its being pure. They'd think it came right out of your nice clean kitchen."

"They'd trust it with your face pictured on it," agreed Willard.

"The boys are right," chimed in their mother.

Mama said slowly, "Oh, Adelina, there's Silas to reckon with on this. Remember, he's just now come over to your side by sending over the grain alcohol for the solvent."

"Yes, there is Silas to reckon with, all right." Aunt Adelina was frowning now and biting her lower lip. "I think he might not mind my trying to sell the tonic—but my name and face on the label. Those are horses of another color!"

"What color?" demanded Zenobia.

"Hush up, child," ordered her mother.

"What shall I do? Shall I put my face on the label?" I saw how my aunt was looking up at the ceiling, so I braced myself by grabbing hold of the kitchen table. Mama, who had turned paler, was doing the same thing.

The sound the two of us had expected came almost the instant the words left Aunt Adelina's mouth. It wasn't a bang this time. It was a crashing overhead as if somebody had dropped a blacksmith's anvil on the floor of the upstairs room directly over the kitchen. I truly shivered with the willies this time, for that room was my bedroom.

"Thank you," said my aunt, turning to the Apley brothers, who were gaping at the ceiling. "I'll go along with your idea as long as your sketch of me, Willard, isn't too dreadful."

The twins smiled at her, nodded together, and shook each other's hand. They had thought she was thanking them for their suggestion, but I knew better.

Mrs. Apley asked, while her sons went off to talk together in a corner, "Missus, is this house settling or something? Or is there somebody upstairs dropping things on the floor?"

I rescued all of us from embarrassment. "That was only some books I piled up on a bookshelf falling down on the floor in my bedroom."

Willard proved to be a good pen-and-ink sketcher. That same afternoon he posed Aunt Adelina in the parlor dressed in her best gown and a Spanish comb in her hair. He sketched her while Mama played on the cottage organ. The tunes my aunt kept asking for, while the Apleys and we Howards watched Willard, were "Onward Christian Soldiers" and "The Battle Hymn of the Republic." I thought I knew why. They were to put her in the proper frame of mind for Uncle Silas.

As soon as the ink had dried, Willard took the portrait, which made Aunt Adelina look stern but intelligent, off to the printer, saying he'd do the hand-lettering at the printers' and that he'd have two sizes of labels made. He and Victor would paste the small labels on the sample bottles and leave the bigger ones with Aunt Adelina for later.

When Mrs. Apley and her girls had gone, I asked my aunt, "When do you plan to tell Uncle Silas?"

"I have decided not to tell him at all, Lucinda. I plan to leave one of the tonic labels on top of his newspaper and let him find out that way."

"What do you think he'll do?" asked Mama.

"I have no idea, Cassie. I think at this moment Silas could do just about anything."

"But he repented and bought the alcohol for you, Aunt Adelina," I said.

She got up, smoothed out her dark-blue silk skirts, and told me, "I don't want to discuss that now. I'm going upstairs to lie down with a vinegar-soaked cloth on my forehead. All this has given me a headache. Those Apley twins come on full chisel so much of the time that they wear me out. I look forward to their leaving Denton, so there'll be some peace and quiet for a while. The way things look I'll be my own best customer for the elixir."

*   *   *

I found out the next day when I came home from school how Uncle Silas had taken to things. Mama told me because Aunt Adelina was upstairs again with a vinegar-soaked cloth on her forehead.

Uncle Silas had spotted the label immediately that morning when he'd come into the parlor to read his *Oregonian* at eight o'clock. He'd let out a bellow that had sent Mama flying up to her room and Aunt Adelina flying into the parlor. First he'd yelled and ranted, and then there had been a deathly silence. Mama heard him clumping upstairs and the noise of dresser drawers and the closet door being opened. Afterward she'd heard him clumping downstairs and the sound of the front door slamming.

"He has moved out on Adelina. He says she has disgraced the Westlake name and him by letting her face be put on a bottle and displayed in public places."

"Where did he go?" I asked.

"To the Payday Saloon. Your aunt says that he plans to rent a room over it. He told her that Gus Heffer will understand how cruelly women can deal with men."

Thunderation! "Oh, my, do you think Uncle Silas will turn Heffer against Mrs. Apley?"

"I don't know, Lucinda. All I know is that it's a terrible situation we're in."

I asked, "Can Aunt Adelina stop Victor and Willard?"

"No, it's too late. It seems they worked all night getting sample bottles filled. Then they divided the little labels among themselves to paste on later, filled carpetbags, and left town. Victor took the train to Portland and Willard the stagecoach to points south. Their mother gave them some money."

The Apley twins had taken the bit in their teeth. They were off and running already.

I got up and went out to the kitchen, where I took not one, but two tablespoonfuls of the green elixir. My spirits needed lifting. After all, that's what it was supposed to do—lift a person. When I'd swallowed the last one and put down the spoon, I looked up at the ceiling and couldn't stop the shiver that came over me. I would never get used to him.

I soon learned that my aunt had no intention of going to the Payday Saloon to try to coax Uncle Silas back home. She didn't even have any intention of writing him a note asking him to come back.

She told Mama, Henry Frederick, and me, "Silas can cool his heels and his temper at the Payday until the cows come home as far as I am concerned. He can eat wherever he chooses, but we shall continue to do his laundry. He says that I have humbled him in Denton by going into business and showing my face in public." She sniffed. "As if women in 1874 are supposed to wear veils, as they do in India! I am going to see to it that he has clean shirts and underwear so that he will not humble *me* in Denton. Lucinda and Henry Frederick will carry the laundry to and from the Payday."

I said, "Aunt Adelina, I don't want to go into a saloon!"

Mama said, "I forbid either of my children to do that."

"They won't have to, Cassie. There is an outside staircase behind the saloon leading to the room Silas is staying in."

My brother put in, "That's right. I've been back there, and I've seen it."

"Thank you, Henry Frederick. Well, to go on, there is a bell on the back porch of the saloon. Ladies who come buying wine for supper parties and beer for their husbands ring it once to get Mr. Heffer or one of his bartenders to come out back. Silas said that two pulls on that same bell will bring him downstairs, if he's in his room."

My brother said to me, "One for Heffer, two for Uncle Silas. I can remember that, but I'm too busy to go."

I flared at him, "I suppose you can't go because you spend all your time hanging over the pigpens. I doubt if you can get your mind off pigs for more than five minutes at a time!" He and Victor had had a long talk at our sty before Victor had left town.

"I keep telling you that hogs are very interesting animals, Lucinda. Pigs are a lot more interesting than those old laying hens you've given names to. It seems to me that in a lot of ways pigs are more like people than chickens are."

I ignored him for the rest of that evening, after Mama had told him that we had heard enough about pigs for one night. How could he think pigs were more interesting than chickens? Why, every hen in our hen house was almost a person to me. I just didn't understand Henry Frederick at all these days.

That next Saturday Aunt Adelina sent me to the Payday Saloon because neither she nor Mama could pry Henry Frederick from the pigsty, and he insisted that he had to go over to the Apley sty right after he was through slopping our hogs.

I wasn't eager to go to the saloon in the rain, but I did,

carrying a wicker basket with an oilcloth cover over it. The basket had two clean shirts in it and some collars and a suit of clean long underwear. I was to bring the basket back full of dirty clothes, if Uncle Silas would give them up.

As I left, I asked Aunt Adelina, "What am I supposed to say to Uncle Silas about how things are here at home?"

She told me very firmly, "In case he asks, you are to say that we are doing simply splendidly."

"But we aren't! Oh well, all right." I'd caught the look on her face. She wasn't to be trifled with at this instant.

So I was supposed to fib to him. We weren't doing at all splendidly. Aunt Adelina looked to me as if she wasn't sleeping. There were big dark circles under her eyes, which hadn't been there before Uncle Silas had walked out on her. Well, I'd better say what she told me to, if I planned to get along with her. I knew she was plenty worried about the payment due on the Bradshaw debt at the bank, and she had Uncle Silas to worry about too. Now that I'd had some time to ponder it, I didn't think it was so wicked of her to have her face on the tonic label. After all, it was her tonic, not anybody else's.

Being careful I didn't get the underwear and shirts wet, I walked to the Payday Saloon and around through the mud to the back door. I peered up through the drizzle, searching for the bell. There it was nailed at one side of the door, with a knotted cord hanging down from it. I grabbed the cord and gave it two hard pulls, then waited, looking up at the staircase for Uncle Silas to come down.

He didn't come. So I pulled again the bell. Was he still asleep? It was nearly noon.

Then all at once the saloon back door opened and out came Mr. Heffer. "Why, it's the little Howard girl. I take it you've come here looking for Si Westlake."

"Yes, sir, I did."

"He ain't here, little lady. He's gone fishing on the river. He won't be back till late. I know him and his ways when he goes fishing."

I said, "Oh." Then I asked, "Could you please give this basket to him when he comes back? It's got his clean shirts and long underwear in it."

"Sure, come on inside out of the rain."

Thunderation, but this was embarrassing, so embarrassing that I decided for the sake of Mrs. Apley's romance and Uncle Silas's friendship with him that I'd better go into the back room, even if Mama would hate hearing about it. And, of course, I had always hankered to see what a saloon back room looked like.

So I said, "Maybe I'd better get in out of the rain, so I don't catch la grippe."

The back room of the Payday was disappointing. There wasn't anybody at all in it but the two of us, and there wasn't any furniture but plain, round wooden tables and unpainted chairs. There weren't any glasses or whiskey bottles or playing cards in sight either. The only picture in the room was a painting of a buck deer crashing through the underbrush with a cougar and three wolves chasing him.

"Sit down. You're Lucy, ain't you?"

"No, I'm Lucinda, Mr. Heffer. Lucy is what that Victor Apley calls me. But it isn't my name."

"You don't like being called Lucy?"

"No, sir, I like my own name. I think Victor calls me that just to get my goat, and he gets it, all right."

He was smiling now. "I guess you don't take to Victor."

"No, sir, to tell you the truth I don't, not the way my brother, Henry Frederick, does. He and Victor have hogs in common."

"That's what I figured at your aunt's supper party," Heffer said, as he sat down across from me. "I could have a bottle of sarsaparilla brought in here if you'd like."

"I better not have any, thank you all the same. Mama wouldn't like it if the word got around Denton that I was drinking in a saloon."

He chuckled. "Nobody will ever know. I'll have some with you." And he got up and went to the door to call for sarsaparilla and *washed* glasses for the back-room customers.

Over the sarsaparilla a bartender in a clean, white apron brought us, Heffer told me, "You know, Lucinda, I never took much to that Victor either. I've some cause to believe that he and his twin brother switched off working for me one day before Victor upped and quit on me. It was queer the way Victor all at once forgot his chores after he'd done them so often."

I said, "That could be. I'll bet those two have switched like that before. It isn't nice of them and not polite either." I took a swig of my sweet-tasting drink and asked, "How do you like Mrs. Apley?"

"She's a comely little lady. I look forward to taking her and her gals to the circus."

Hearing this warmed and emboldened me, so I went on to say, "She dotes on you. I overheard her tell Mama and Aunt Adelina she half swoons when she hears your name spoken, and she thinks you have the most handsome moustache in Denton."

"Does she now?" He was touching his drooping moustache tenderly.

"Mr. Heffer, I think you ought to get to know her and make an impression on her fast, before some man marries her. Mrs. Apley's going to be a rich lady pretty soon. She's gone into business with my Aunt Adelina. I bet you didn't know that. It's been a sort of secret till now, but I'll tell you anyhow. Willard and Victor are working in the business, too."

Heffer shook his head at me. "Well, you do seem to be up on things and plainspoken, too, to hint that I'd take up with a lady because she might become rich. That ain't why I'm escorting Mrs. Apley to the circus. I like her and her little gals. I don't want her money. You told me a secret just now, so I'll tell you one. It's something nobody knows, and I'm only telling it to you because it appears to me that a surprise would do you some good, little miss know-it-all. It so happens that I'm part owner of your aunt's elixir business, and I have high hopes of its being a success. Mrs. Westlake impressed me as a forceful female, a mighty good woman to want to help out the family fortunes the way she's doing. I wonder why Silas acts the way he does. I'm proud to be Adelina Westlake's partner."

A light blazed in my head. That handshake in the parlor after supper was a business handshake. Mr. Heffer had agreed to become Aunt Adelina's partner!

I asked, "Does Uncle Silas know about your being a partner?"

"Nope. Your aunt asked me not to tell him because it

would upset him when he's worried about his business troubles at the bank. Besides it might cost me my friendship with him. He doesn't know that I'm supplying all the alcohol, and when the time comes I'll be sending over the corks and empty bottles your aunt's going to be needing."

Thunderation, that explained the keg of alcohol for the tonic solvent! "I tasted the new green tonic, and it's fine," I said.

"I'm happy to hear that, Lucinda. Now, you better not tattle to your uncle about being a partner of your aunt's. I want to be a secret partner—an extremely secret one."

"I won't tattle. And I'm glad you're a partner. I'm proud that you told me, and I'll keep the secret. I hope you make lots of money, too, along with Aunt Adelina and Mrs. Apley. Well, I'd better get along home now. Thank you for the sarsaparilla."

I got up, leaving the basket on the table, and went out to the back door. Mr. Heffer followed me. On the bottom step I told him, "I'll come here Monday after school and pick up my uncle's dirty laundry. Please tell him that, and will you tell him, too, that Aunt Adelina wants him to be sure to change his long underwear every week and put it in with his dirty shirts and socks and handkerchiefs?"

"I'll be sure to tell him." Heffer sounded very mournful to me as he said, "Si Westlake is a lucky man to have all you ladies so concerned about his dirty socks."

This was my chance, and I took it. "My aunt is pretty good at doing laundry work, but Mrs. Apley beats her all hollow. You ought to see how she irons a shirt. She can iron rings around my mother." That wasn't true. Mama was a fine ironer, but I figured I'd best remember how taken Heffer had been with Mama at supper that night. Mrs. Apley was the one he was supposed to court.

I waved at him and started off through the rain. As I trotted down the boardwalk past the Denton Bank, I stuck my tongue out at it. Mr. Heffer's secret that he had joined forces with Aunt Adelina certainly had put more heart into me. I only wished I could tell Mama what I knew, but that was Aunt Adelina's business, not mine.

I went back to the Payday's back door next Monday afternoon, just as I'd said I would, and this time after I pulled the bell two times, Uncle Silas came down with the basket.

I asked, "Did you change your underwear and your shirt?"

"Yes, I did. You tell your aunt that I promise to do this faithfully."

"Sure." As I took the basket from him, I asked, "Did you catch any fish Saturday?"

"I caught some trout. I fried them up for Gus and me."

I said, "You know, you don't appear to look so good, Uncle Silas. Didn't the trout agree with your stomach?" I thought he looked a bit bloated.

"I don't feel too well at that, Lucinda, but it isn't the fish. It's all my troubles—your aunt's stubborn attitude about that label business and the debt falling due at the bank."

"Mr. Bradshaw's three-hundred-dollar debt?"

"That's right. There aren't many days left to go now before I have to come up with the money. If I can't raise it, Lambertson will force us to sell the house. I'm trying to scrape it up by collecting from men who owe me, but they haven't got the money either." He leaned down to ask me softly, "Would you ask your Aunt Adelina if she'd let me have that lapel watch of hers to sell, only temporarily?"

"You mean the gold one with the little diamonds set on the case?" I was so startled and flustered to hear him ask for it when he'd refused to take it once before that a dreadful thing happened. The words popped out of me. "Oh, but she's already pawned it in a pawnshop in Portland to get money for the tonic. They gave her twenty dollars for it." I slapped my hand over my big blurting mouth, but it was too late.

"Oh, my Lord," was all he said. Then he turned around and went upstairs, holding onto the railing all the way to the top.

I stood where I was with the basket until I saw the door of the upstairs room shut behind him. He'd caught me flat-footed with his question. *I had tattled!* Thunderation, this was the last thing in the world that I had wanted to do, to make more trouble between him and Aunt Adelina. Why hadn't I thought to say that the minute hand was stuck and the watch was being repaired?

Uncle Silas had truly looked poorly. He had the same dark circles under his eyes that Aunt Adelina had. He wasn't sleeping well either, but then how could he? Saloons were very noisy places after dark, full of loud talkers and piano music.

Well, I supposed in some ways Aunt Adelina was better off than he was. Poplar Street was quiet, and she was taking her wonder-working tonic every day.

I made up my mind to do a good deed the next Monday I came back. I'd ask Aunt Adelina to let me bring some of the tonic to perk up Uncle Silas. And while I was at it, I'd fetch some for Mr. Heffer, too. If he was a partner, even a silent one, he ought to dose himself with it to see if he approved. I certainly didn't want either one of them to come down with la grippe—especially Mr. Heffer, who needed all his strength for courting.

CHAPTER VIII

The Weak Sister

I decided not to tell Aunt Adelina that he'd asked about her lapel watch because hearing it would only make her more unhappy. I knew she couldn't go up to Portland to get it back since she didn't have the money yet. I knew, too, because I'd overheard her talking with Mrs. Apley, that she didn't want to take more cash from her. After all, Mrs. Apley's sons, Victor and Willard, had set out as unpaid drummers, traveling to sell the tonic.

A week went by with no word from Uncle Silas for Aunt Adelina or from the Apley twins to anybody. I helped Aunt Adelina and Mrs. Apley make a bigger batch of the green tonic from the two kegs of grain alcohol that had come over by rented wagon from the Payday Saloon.

I hadn't said a word, while I helped stir one of the pots to keep the roots and herbs from scorching, when Mrs. Apley exclaimed to my aunt, "Oh, missus, I think it's just grand the way Silas keeps sending over what we need for the wet part of the tonic, even if he claims to be mad at you."

"Yes, it is," said my aunt, not looking up from her mortar.

"But it appears to me to be mighty strange," Mrs. Apley said, "that he don't come back home to live. Missus, he can't be mad at you anymore over the label if he sends the liquor to you, can he?"

My aunt told her, "Eleanora, I do not pretend to understand menfolks much of the time, do you?"

Mrs. Apley giggled. "There's one man I think I understand, missus. That sweet, dear, little Gus Heffer and me got along like milk and honey when he took us to the circus Tuesday evening. He dotes on my gals, and they dote on him. He walked around the elephants holding hands with Zenobia on one side of him and Yolanda on the other. He's asked me out Saturday night to supper and a melodrama at the theater later."

My aunt stopped with her pestle in midair and said, "Excellent, Eleanora. What do you two talk about?"

"About the tonic sometimes, but mostly about how awful lonesome he is, and how lonesome I am now that Victor and Willard are gone. Mr. Heffer seemed tickled to hear that they were out seeing the world. He told me that they were plenty old enough to be making their own way. He was doing that when he was fourteen."

I said, "That's pretty young, isn't it?"

"Not the way Gus sees it. He thinks thirteen's about the

right age for a young man to start doing things on his own."

Frowning, Aunt Adelina said, "All right, ladies, it's time for me to put in the secret ingredient, a pinch of it in each pot. I must ask you to leave the kitchen while I do this. Count to ninety out in the hallway, please, and then come back. It takes only a minute or so."

Out in the hallway, Mrs. Apley asked me, "What's the secret thing, Lucinda?" Then she started to count under her breath in a whisper.

"I don't know what it is, but I think she bought it in a little pharmacy on Jefferson Street in Portland. She brought it home in her black-beaded reticule, so it must be very small."

Mrs. Apley nodded, as she went on to eighty in the count. Then I asked her, "Do you think we ought to try to sell the tonic in Denton, too?"

"You bet I do. Victor says that in time it's going to sell here, but he figured he'd start your aunt's wonder-working tonic elsewhere, to get up a head of steam to impress Denton."

I said, "I think it's too bad that it isn't sold here in Aunt Adelina's hometown first. I'll bet it hurts her feelings."

"I suspect it does, Lucinda. It sure hurts mine, but what can we do about it now?"

All I could do was nod, but at the same time I was thinking maybe there was something more I could do to help my aunt than just stand over a stove, stirring.

I tried to be helpful that next Monday afternoon when I headed out in a light downpour for the Payday with the laundry basket. The basket held two little bottles of the green tonic, along with the clean long underwear and two shirts.

I handed Uncle Silas the basket. "There's some tonic here for you and Mr. Heffer, to keep you from getting la grippe. Will you see to it that he gets his bottle, please? Last time I talked with him he told me he'd like to see how it tastes. If you'll put your dirty clothes in here, I'll be on my way now. I have some other errands to do today."

He gave me a nod, took the basket, went upstairs, and came right back down with it. He asked, "How's your aunt, Lucinda?"

"She's splendid, Uncle Silas," I fibbed. Then I said, eyeing him, "I think maybe you're losing weight, and you've gone grayer in the beard and eyebrows than you were last week."

"That wouldn't surprise me, child. It's what comes from female willfulness. Your aunt is full of what is willful these days. Gus and I take turns doing the cooking here at night. We aren't too good at it. I take it that you'll be back here again next Monday?"

"Yes, sir, to bring you clean clothes. Good luck on getting the money to pay off the bank."

"Thank you, Lucinda. Luck is what I need, all right."

I was even more worried now that I'd seen Uncle Silas and wanted more than ever to help Aunt Adelina, so I gritted my teeth hard to get my courage up and went into the Denton Pharmacy to talk to the owner. I wasn't there long. Next, I braced myself again, threw back my shoulders, and walked to Quincy's General Store, where I talked for a short time to the owner. Finally, I went across the street to the emporium and had an even shorter conversation with the man there.

Though said in different words, I heard the same discouraging thing at all three places: "No, I'm sorry, but I don't know anything about Mrs. Westlake's Wonder-Working Elixir, though I've sure heard from a number of folks in town about her hair restorer and face powder and other things. No, I don't think I can stock your aunt's medicine in my shebang."

I felt daunted and bruised as I headed for home, but still I had tried to help out. Nobody in Denton, at least as far as I was concerned, seemed to want the green wonder-worker. It surely went against my grain to admit it to myself, but Victor Apley seemed to be dead right about Denton.

The Reverend Curley, who was a tall man with gray hair and no beard, came all at once out of the rain toward me down the boardwalk, walking with his wife. He tipped his hat to me. "How are you today, Lucinda Lavina?"

"I guess I'm all right, Mr. Curley, even if I'm getting wet and weary." Then I told him, "You are absolutely right in what you said last Easter in your sermon about a prophet not getting any honor in his own hometown. I just wanted you to know that I think you said the right and true thing."

"Well, Lucinda, it's nice to learn that people listen to my sermons."

"They surely do listen. They're very interested in what you say, and they hope you'll stay for years and years here in Denton."

What I said was true enough, yet he wasn't smiling all the way across his face the way he should to hear such a nice thing. He was looking a bit washed out.

I asked Mrs. Curley, "Are you giving your husband a tonic nowadays?"

"No, she is not!" Mr. Curley shook his head at me.

"He doesn't like the way they taste, Lucinda," his wife explained.

I nodded at both of them. "I know. That's because of the sulphur that goes into most tonics. We don't take that sort of tonic anymore, thank heaven. Aunt Adelina Westlake makes a special one for us that tastes just fine. Aren't we lucky to have such a smart and clever aunt?"

I left the Curleys after I'd said, "Good day." If I waited around, I would only give them time to ask me questions about how things were going in our house. I suspected that they knew about our money troubles from talking to the Lambertsons, who, I knew for a fact, had already told the minister about Aunt Adelina's being a spiritualist. I certainly didn't want to have to discuss the dismaying Mr. Whitlow with him.

On my way home I saw some Westlake family friends, and I told them, too, that I thought they might like to try out a new spring tonic someday soon. My hope was to get them into the right frame of mind to buy our tonic when it finally got into the Denton stores. After all, something I had said may have helped Mrs. Apley's and Mr. Heffer's romance along. Telling him that "love was winging on its way to him" might have proved helpful. Kind words could help out a great deal in a person's life. I would have been a lot happier that day if I had heard yes three times instead of three no's.

I decided not to tell Aunt Adelina about my visits to the stores or about my trying to talk people into buying the tonic. These days I had to be pretty careful of what I said when I tried to sell her products.

Mrs. Apley was in the kitchen talking to both Aunt Adelina and Mama when I returned. It seemed to me that she was so happy she was going to explode. She was waving her hands and flitting about the kitchen, first grabbing and kissing Zenobia, then Yolanda. Because I thought she might be about to make a hugging grab at me, I put the basket in front of my chest and drew back to the door.

"Oh, Lucinda," she sang out. "Mr. Heffer said yes when him and me got home Saturday night from the melodrama."

"What did he say yes to?" All at once I thought I knew and I gasped. She had popped the question. *She* had proposed to *him*! Ladies never did the proposing as far as I knew. It was unheard of.

"He invited me to become his blushing bride when Zenobia asked him to marry me."

"Zenobia?" I gawked at the youngest girl.

"Uh-huh, I asked him to ask her," she said.

"Zenobia certainly did," put in Aunt Adelina, smiling.

Yolanda explained. "My sister asked Mr. Heffer why he kept Ma out so late at night and didn't he think it was time he was our pa."

"And then Gus popped the question—out on the front steps under my umbrella, which was where he took me to ask me quietlike." Mrs. Apley flung her arms wide. "I'm so happy, so very happy. We'll be tieing the knot before long. Gus is going up to Portland today to get the rings—the biggest ruby engagement ring in town and a gold wedding ring, he says. And once I've got that ruby on my finger, the next thing I'm gonna do is send for my boy Xerxes."

"Zurkcees?" I spelled it out loud, "Z-u-r-k-c-e-e-s?"

"No, no, Lucinda. X-e-r-x-e-s! Xerxes X-a-v-i-e-r."

"Eleanora, where has *this* boy been?" asked my aunt.

"Up in Canada, in Ontario, with my late husband's ma. She's too old and feeble now to care properly for him anymore."

I had to know. "Is he a triplet or just a twin?"

"Neither one, Lucinda. Xerxes comes in line after Victor and Willard. He's sixteen."

Aunt Adelina asked, "Eleanora, what do you propose to do with Xerxes when he gets here?"

"Feed him and love him, like I do all the others." She scooped up Zenobia and Yolanda, who were struggling and kicking, and kissed them on the cheeks.

My aunt said, "I think it would be wisest if you wrote Xerxes to stay where he is until Victor and Willard come back to let us know how things go with the tonic."

"All right, I'll do that, but it goes against my heart." And then she sailed happily out the kitchen door, and I heard her helping her girls into their oilskins.

When she'd gone, I sat down and said, "I brought back the dirty laundry. Uncle Silas looks peaked and says he doesn't like his and Mr. Heffer's cooking. I guess you hadn't heard of Xerxes before either, huh?"

"Indeed not," answered my mother. "I think it would be most unwise of Eleanora to have him show up now. It didn't seem to me at our supper party that Mr. Heffer took to Victor and Willard the way he does to the girls."

I said, "He does seem to favor girls. I know for a fact that he doesn't take much to the twins. I think he's very glad they're big enough to be out on their own."

"Yes, I suspect you are right, but he does like Zenobia and Yolanda." Aunt Adelina was biting her lower lip, which meant to me that she was upset about something. She raised her eyes to the ceiling and asked out loud, "Should Eleanora bring the boy Xerxes here? Will all go well for her and Mr. Heffer's wedding plans?"

My neck hairs were prickling while I waited and waited. Then came not one but two thudding sounds from the warming oven on top of the stove.

"*Two* of them? What does that mean?" I asked her.

"Mr. Whitlow is saying no, Lucinda."

I said, "Oh, my," along with Mama. Then I asked my aunt, "Does he ever say maybe? What would that sound like?"

She told me firmly, "Mr. Whitlow does not deal in *maybe* or *perhaps*, dear. He knows his own mind."

Feeling dismayed, I went to the back porch to put Uncle Silas's dirty clothes in the copper tub to soak, before they got boiled on top of the stove. These days our laundry sometimes soaked and soaked and soaked before the stove top was clear of tonic pots. As I dumped the long underwear in the tub, I was telling myself that I was very glad Mr. Whitlow had given up dropping anvils in my bedroom. Those oven thuds were much nicer. But what was to go wrong with the wedding plans? I wondered.

Another week went by almost to its very end, and it was peaceful as far as I was concerned, except that I still was not talking to Caralee. She wouldn't give an inch on what she'd said, and neither would I. When Miss Hinkle wanted to know why we stayed apart at recess, I said I was suffering from toothaches, and Caralee said she was having stomach-aches.

There was one interesting thing, though. Mr. Heffer got back from Portland with the rings. I didn't get to see the wedding ring because he kept that, but I couldn't miss the ruby. It was big and round and red as a red-hot coal on Mrs. Apley's finger. I wondered if he had told her when he gave her the ruby that he was a secret partner in the tonic business.

I decided that it was all too much for me, and I was weary of thinking the way grown-ups did. But to become familiar with the sort of books that interested them, I started reading Uncle Silas's copy of essays by Ralph Waldo Emerson. They weren't much like *The Man in the Iron Mask*, but because Caralee wasn't speaking to me she wasn't lending me any of her books either. Anyway, Ralph Waldo Emerson was very uplifting, and sometimes I thought I understood what he was driving at.

Thunderation, but life had become troublesome.

It got more so on that next Monday when Victor came back. Was he ever excited when he came bounding through the rain up onto our front veranda. "Mrs. Westlake, hey, Mrs. Westlake," he called out. "It's me, Victor Apley, and I've got some good news. Just as soon as I go see your pigs, I'll come tell you all about it. Where's Henry Fred now?"

Mama, who had answered the doorbell, told Victor, "Henry Frederick is, alas, where he usually is these days, out behind the house with his pigs."

Victor didn't even wait for Aunt Adelina to come to the

front door. He was gone, running around the side of the house. My aunt said, "Well, I never! That young man seems more concerned with pigs than with people, doesn't he?"

I told her, "Oh, he'll be back." I was all too sure of that.

Ten minutes later Victor did come back, to the back door this time. While he devoured the deviled-egg sandwich that Mama made him, he told us that he'd gotten orders for tonic in lots of places. Men who owned general stores and pharmacies thought it looked fine, smelled good, and tasted all right for a tonic. They thought that a lady's face on the label was a dandy idea, and they were certain they could sell it to their lady customers."

Victor finished with, "So you make up some more batches of it, and I'll see that they get to their destinations by wagon or railroad. The wonder-worker is going to catch on. I plan to sell it for the first year at seventy-five cents a bottle, then at a whole dollar. Don't you ladies worry. We're on our way." He got up, wiped his hands on the tablecloth, and said, "I better get on home now and see Ma and the girls and find out whether Ma's heard from Willard. What's new hereabouts, Lucy?"

I answered him with no hesitation, "Uncle Silas got so mad when he heard that Aunt Adelina's face is on the tonic label that he moved out to a room in the Payday Saloon. Your mother's engaged to be married to Mr. Heffer, who we're scared won't take to the idea that his bride-to-be wants to bring another Apley here—your brother Xerxes. Aunt Adelina and your mother and I are keeping busy making tonic here because we keep getting alcohol from the Payday Saloon, and when I'm not helping them, I'm taking clean long underwear to Uncle Silas and reading Ralph Waldo Emerson's essays. And my name is Lucinda, not Lucy."

His mouth was hanging open. I'd finally gotten him, all right. So I went on to say, "Henry Frederick's practically moved in with our pigs and your pigs these days. What have you done to him? He does everything but hold umbrellas over them. And please remember that my name is Lucinda!"

"*Lucinda!*" came from Mama.

Victor turned to Mama. "Mrs. Howard, are you making the tonic, too?"

"No, Cassie isn't," replied Aunt Adelina. "She's cleaning the house and doing the cooking and laundry and playing the cottage organ to spur us on with inspiring music."

"Oh, so she's not making the wonder-worker, huh? She's spurring, while you other ladies are stirring. To my way of thinking that makes her the weak sister."

I knew those evil words *weak sister*. I'd heard them before. They meant somebody feeble—sort of poor-relations feeble. I looked quickly at Mama, hoping that Victor's insult wouldn't make her weep and run upstairs.

Not this time, though. Thunderation, I'd never seen her act the way she was acting now. There had to be something about Victor Apley that got her dander up also. She got up, snatched away the plate the sandwich had been on, and told him, "I have given my sister, Mrs. Westlake, who is your employer, money to buy ingredients for the tonic, and I have run this household single-handed so that she can give all her time to making the tonic. I have twenty-five dollars remaining to my name. I have offered that cash to her again and again, but she won't take it."

"Take it from her, Mrs. Westlake, take it." Victor was nodding at Mama and my aunt. "I came down here with a pocketful of orders, but danged few merchants advanced me any cash yet. They plan to sell the wonder-worker and give you half of what they make from it. That's how it's going to be until the tonic gets established and folks know it by name and by your face on the bottle. Then the merchants will start to pay you more for each bottle that gets sold. Take that twenty-five dollars. Great things are in store for the elixir and for all of us. I know what I'm talking about. I have my secrets, too, you know."

"Adelina, please take the money," pleaded Mama.

"All right, Cassie, all right. But Victor, don't you ever let me hear you talk to my sister like that again. She is bolder than a lioness when she sets her mind to it. You just saw her. Wasn't she a fearful sight, though?"

"She sure was." He was grinning. "Now I'd better go see our pigs and talk to Ma about things, such as when she plans to get Xerxes down here to Denton. It better be later rather than sooner." And with that he left, going out the back door fast as he could.

"Dear heaven, that young man does wear a person out," were Mama's words.

"True, Cassie, but he sells the elixir. I only hope Victor stays with us long enough to get the tonic established before he goes into the pig-raising business. Did you notice that he went to see the pigs today before he even saw us?"

I told her, "I surely took note of that. I think Henry Frederick's worse, though. He's gone to the pigs all the way these days." I thought this funny remark might cheer them up because sometimes folks said the "world was going to the dogs."

The face my aunt turned on me wasn't a smiling one, though. She looked like her portrait on the label as she muttered, "I do wonder what Willard is doing and how he's doing, wherever he might be at this moment."

Mama put in quietly, "It isn't Willard I wonder about, Adelina. I wonder about this Xerxes Xavier."

We found out about him the next Sunday. Mrs. Apley came over in the afternoon with Zenobia and Yolanda and a short, dark-haired boy wearing a blue suit and copper-toed shoes. He was carrying two carpetbags as he came up to our porch. We guessed who he was even before she opened her mouth to introduce him. She stood beside him beaming with pride. I was pleased to note that he didn't look one bit like Victor or Willard or the girls. I surely hoped he would be different from his older brothers.

I asked, "You're Xerxes, aren't you?"

"Yes, ma'am." He sort of bowed to me and even took off his hat. Certainly he had much better manners than Victor or Willard. "Yes, I am Xerxes Xavier Apley," he added. His accent was different, too.

Mama said, "Oh, you must have just got off the train."

"What makes you think that, missus?" asked Mrs. Apley.

"Because of the carpetbags he's carrying, Eleanora," explained my aunt.

"Oh, them. They don't mean much. Xerxes got to Denton last evening. He came down by wagon. The girls and I fussed over him a bit before we brought him over here to live with you folks."

"To live with us?" Mama let out a small cry.

"I got to thinking about what you folks had said about dear little Gus maybe not taking to the idea of my having another boy, when Gus is so partial to gals. So my idea was to bring Xerxes here and pass him off as Xerxes Westlake, some kin of your husband's, since Silas doesn't live here anymore. It won't be for very long. When I think the time has come for me to tell Gus about Xerxes, I'll do it, and Xerxes can come home and live with all of us."

Thunderation, what an idea! Aunt Adelina and Mama were gaping at each other like two barn owls caught in a thunderstorm.

"But Eleanora, Silas has no family back East anymore. He has no family anywhere at all," said my aunt.

"No matter, missus. Your Silas won't find out. He's not here. You'll take to my Xerxes. He's clean in his habits, he's got good manners, and he's quiet as a mouse and a jim-dandy reader. He takes after his papa's ma, who was a Canadian schoolmarm. Xerxes will help you with the tonic, too, won't you, Xerxes?"

"All right, Mother, I'll help." I saw how he smiled at us, not at her.

He truly wasn't one bit like his brothers at all. I could tell that Aunt Adelina was impressed with him, and so was Mama. They were smiling quite fondly at him.

"All right, Eleanora," said my aunt after a time. "If Xerxes will make himself useful around the house, we'll take him in and pass him off as a Westlake, though it is a dreadful lie."

"Thank you. You won't be sorry you took Xerxes in."

* * *

Xerxes, who told me he was named after an old-time king of Persia, was helpful as his mother had said. He'd been well trained by his grandmother in Canada. Quiet and courteous, he even helped me do the dishes.

Henry Frederick didn't like him, though, because he was too much of a gent. The second night Xerxes was in our house my brother told me that he didn't fancy sharing a room with him, and the only reason he did was because Mama wasn't above using a hairbrush on the seat of his pants. Finally Henry Frederick asked me in a very sour manner, "What do you suppose Uncle Silas would say about Xerxes Apley's being here, Lucinda?"

I told him, "If Uncle Silas were here at home where he belongs, trying to help Aunt Adelina, who may be killing herself with overwork, he would have the right to say plenty. But he isn't here. He doesn't even come to the house, and don't you dare call him Xerxes *Apley*. Remember that he's a *Westlake*. And pray that Uncle Silas doesn't show up here unexpectedly."

"I hope Uncle Silas does, Lucinda. He's having the wool pulled over his eyes."

"Don't you dare go to the Payday and tell him about Xerxes!"

"You won't have to worry, Lucinda. I don't have it in mind to do that. But Uncle Silas might come here all on his own. After all, it's his house, too."

My prayers that Uncle Silas would stay at the Payday weren't answered. Four days after Xerxes had moved in, Uncle Silas came home and found Xerxes sitting in the parlor with me, looking at our slides of reindeer and Laplanders.

I didn't know who was opening the door at first, and I certainly wasn't expecting Uncle Silas. Mama had gone out on an errand to Mrs. Apley's with some more Oregon grape roots for the tonic she was making, so I thought it was Mama and I called out, "We're in here."

Then in came Uncle Silas, who had just taken off his mackintosh. His first words to me the instant after he'd spotted Xerxes were, "Who's that on the settee with you, Lucinda?"

"Xerxes Westlake," said Xerxes Apley right away.

"Xerxes Westlake?" How puzzled Uncle Silas looked.

I was speechless with horror as Xerxes went on, "Yes, sir, I'm a relation of Mr. Silas Westlake, Lucinda's uncle. He isn't here right now."

"Oh, yes, he is," said Uncle Silas very loudly. He came forward to peer into Xerxes's face. "I don't have any family anywhere in this country, so who in the devil are you, my boy and what in the devil are you doing here in my house?"

Xerxes got up and discreetly left the room. "I can explain it all to you, if you'll please sit down and listen, Mr. Westlake. It isn't anything to get angry about, sir."

"Isn't it?" Uncle Silas shouted. "A man comes home to his own house for his Congress gaiters and finds it infested with strangers posing as his relatives."

I took a hand in matters at this point, even if I had to shriek to do so. "Uncle Silas, Xerxes isn't a stranger. He's an Apley. He's Mrs. Apley's third son, the one who was living up in Canada till just recently."

"Another Apley?" Uncle Silas sat down where Xerxes had just been sitting.

"Yes," I answered.

"But what is he doing here in this house?"

"He's living here as a Westlake so Mr. Heffer won't know he's an Apley. Aunt Adelina and Mrs. Apley and Mama are scared that Gus Heffer won't like it if another Apley shows up. He might call the wedding off."

Uncle Silas heaved a very deep sigh. "Oh, Lord, poor little Gus. The wool is being pulled over his eyes for sure."

He would have said more except that at that moment Aunt Adelina came into the parlor from the kitchen. Either Xerxes had warned her, or she'd heard me shrieking. She said, "Oh, Silas, it's nice to see you again. I am sorry about Xerxes. We didn't mean to deceive you."

Uncle Silas got to his feet. "No, Adelina, but you meant to deceive poor Gus Heffer. You have it in mind to run another Apley kid in on him. I'm going right back to the Payday as soon as I get my Congress gaiters and tell Gus there's another Apley here."

"No, Silas, you'd better not do that," said Aunt Adelina, who folded her arms over her chest and looked stern, the way she did for the tonic-label sketch.

"And why not, woman?"

"Because if Gus Heffer gets angry with the Apleys or with me, we are all going to be a lot worse off than we are right now."

He snorted at her. "How can that be, Adelina?"

"Very simple, Silas. Mr. Heffer owns one quarter of my elixir business. He supplies the alcohol and will supply the empty bottles and the corks."

"*Gus!* He's stabbed me in the back, too." Uncle Silas sat down again, shaking his head.

"Silas, I couldn't help Xerxes's coming down here to Denton. It wasn't my idea. It was Eleanora's. She wants her sons with her. So would I, if you and I had ever had children." All at once my aunt put her arms out to him. "Silas, Eleanora and the Apleys and I need your help now very badly. Though the twins claim to be good salesmen, and Victor has brought in one hundred and twenty orders for the tonic, they are only boys. Eleanora and I don't know anything about how to sell. Come back home, please, and help me manage the business."

Uncle Silas sank down further and locked his fingers together over his stomach.

I was amazed at the change in Aunt Adelina's behavior. She must have missed Uncle Silas more than she had ever let on, or perhaps Mr. Whitlow had given her a private message to get him back home.

During the quiet between them I said, "I have something to tell both of you. I tried hard as I could to get merchants in Denton to put the tonic in their stores, but they all turned me down. I bet they wouldn't say no to you, Uncle Silas. You're important here in Denton, while I'm only a child."

"You did that, Lucinda, all on your own?" My aunt was staring at me, shaking her head. "My, but that was noble of you."

What I had said seemed to have jolted Uncle Silas, too. He looked up at me. "By Gum, Lucinda, you took it on yourself to do that? It couldn't have been very pleasant."

"It wasn't. I thought I ought to, though. It was a grown-up, helpful thing to do even if it didn't work out. And I'm reading your book of essays of Ralph Waldo Emerson, too, and so is Xerxes. He explains to me what Emerson means."

While Aunt Adelina and I stood waiting, Uncle Silas

moved his hand from his stomach to play with his beard, then he said, "All right. I'll come back home, though I'll never take kindly to the notion of my wife's face being on a bottle. As I see it I've been put upon by my wife and by my best friend and fishing crony, but this house is far more comfortable than that room over the Payday." He looked at me. "And, of course, if I'm here Lucinda won't have to run laundry errands in the rain and risk catching la grippe."

The la grippe epidemic had been over for some time, but all my aunt said was, "You are absolutely right, Silas."

"All right, Adelina. I'll go get my duds and come home tonight."

"You won't tell Mr. Heffer about Xerxes, Silas?"

"No, Adelina. I won't say a word to him about anything. I won't tell him I know that he went into business with you behind my back, but I have to tell you one thing that won't sit so well with you."

"What would that be, Silas?"

"It's this. I'd planned to ask Gus Heffer to lend me one hundred and fifty dollars so I could pay off that debt of Bradshaw's at the bank. It's due in less than a week, remember? I've scraped together one hundred and fifty dollars, because I found a buyer for the carriage, but I don't know where I'm going to find the other half. I won't ask Gus for the money now that I know he's already supplying the alcohol to you for the tonic. I've already asked Lucinda here about your lapel watch, but she's told me what's become of it —that you pawned it."

Oh my! Aunt Adelina had been looking at him, but now she looked straight and hard at me. I knew that I should have told her what had popped out of me that day about the watch. It had been wrong of me not to warn her.

So I said in a sort of wail, "Oh, Aunt Adelina, I'm sorry, but the words just popped out of my mouth."

She sighed, then put her hand on my shoulder as her eyes softened. "That's all right, Lucinda. I forgive you. I should not have burdened you with such a secret in the first place. In fact, I should not have taken you to the pawnshop with me. It wasn't absolutely necessary that you be there or that I tell you what I did inside the shop. It wasn't a proper thing for me to do." She turned her gaze on her husband again. "I am sorry, Silas, but I needed cash very badly then."

"Who doesn't, Adelina?" He was eyeing her hopefully. "You pawned it some time back as I understand it. You haven't got it back yet, have you?" he asked.

Her grip tightened on my shoulder, so I knew she was upset, but her voice was calm as ever as she told him, "No, not yet, Silas. Would you like me to ask Mr. Heffer for the money?"

"No, at least do that much for me, Adelina, to spare my pride. It's my debt, mine and Barlow Bradshaw's—devil take the man wherever he might be. I don't ever want to set eyes on him again."

"All right, Silas. I won't go to Heffer," she promised. "I won't say a word to him about anything except the elixir."

He snorted once more. "Especially about another Apley, huh? I'm sure you won't talk to Gus about that. It appears to me that your friend Mrs. Apley has kids stashed away all over the landscape. A bit sneaky, ain't she, Adelina?"

"I would not use that word, Silas. The poor woman has

done her best all these years as a widow. She has no strong man to help her. She has given of her strength and money to help me in my hour of need. I try to help her in return. What's wrong with that? She loves me and would do just about anything for any one of us."

"Anything for any one of us?" Those words were sticking in my mind after Uncle Silas had left to get his duds at the Payday and move back home.

Because it was only misting outside I didn't put on my oilskins. I threw a shawl of my mother's over my head and hurried out of the house without telling anyone where I was going. I was bent on an errand. Quickly I went to the Apley house, rapped on the door, and was let in by Yolanda.

"I have to see your mama," I told her.

"She's here. She's giving Zenobia a bath in the copper tub out in the kitchen."

"Please ask her to come out here as soon as she can. I need to talk to her alone."

A moment later Mrs. Apley came out, rolling down the sleeves of her calico gown. Her arms were wet and soapy.

"Can we sit down somewhere? I have something to say to you."

"Sure, Lucinda, Zenobia's out of the water now. Take a chair, if you can find an empty one, that is."

I sat down in her tiny parlor and told her about Uncle Silas's moving back and about his finding Xerxes and then finally about Mr. Heffer's being a partner to Aunt Adelina.

She hadn't known this, and her slanting eyes got round with surprise. "Gus, a partner, *too*? Do tell. Ain't that nice! So the liquor came from him—not from your Uncle Silas?"

"That's right." I took a deep breath. "Uncle Silas and Aunt Adelina are in bad trouble, though." And now that I was telling secrets, I told her all about the Bradshaw debt.

"Oh, my, I wish I could help them out."

"You can, Mrs. Apley." This is what I'd hoped she'd say. I took another breath. "Would you take that ruby ring up to Portland to the pawnshop where Aunt Adelina's lapel watch is and pawn it and loan the money to Uncle Silas?"

"Pawn dear Gus's ruby?" She looked astonished that I would ask such a thing.

"Yes'm. You'll get it back. Mr. Heffer will never know."

"But, of course, he'll know, Lucinda Howard. He'll be mad as hops. How'll I keep him from knowing that it's gone off my finger?"

I'd thought about this on my way to her house. "Say that you scalded your left hand making tonic and you'll have to wear a bandage on it until we make enough money to get the ring back."

"Lucinda Lavina!"

"Will you, please? Will you do it?"

"I dunno." She leaned her chin on her fist, thinking.

"It's for my aunt. We could lose our house to the bank if you don't. We'd lose our big kitchen, and our stove holds more elixir pots on top than yours."

"All right, all right. Victor would tell me to do it. I'll go up to Portland with your aunt. She says she needs more roots and herbs and some more of that secret thing, too."

When they returned, Aunt Adelina said Mrs. Apley had gotten a whopping two hundred dollars for the ruby ring at the pawnshop. One hundred and fifty dollars of the money she gave to Aunt Adelina for Uncle Silas.

And I got a scolding from my aunt in front of Mama for "meddling," but later on Mama and Aunt Adelina both gave me a secret hug.

When I asked Aunt Adelina about the lapel watch, she said it had looked just fine hanging on a hook on the pawnshop's wall. She knew for certain she'd be back for it, because there had been a bang in the wall it was hanging on when she'd asked Mr. Whitlow about it in the pawnshop. The pawnbroker had thought it was mice thumping around in the woodwork.

Mama told me what happened the next morning. Later Mrs. Apley came over with her left hand bandaged to the wrist and talked to my uncle privately for a long, long time in the parlor. Uncle Silas went out at one o'clock, shaking his head and muttering about "deceitful females." But all the same he took the money to the Denton Bank and paid off the debt. Our house was safe until the next debt at the bank fell due in July.

We were rid of Mr. Barlow Bradshaw, it seemed, thanks to the kindness of Mrs. Apley, even if we were still looking ruin in the face.

CHAPTER IX

"You Guard That Well, Mrs. Westlake."

We saw the sun now and then for a couple of minutes the first two weeks of April 1874. I remember that well because with all our troubles upon us, the sunshine was most welcome.

Around the middle of the month, a couple of very interesting things happened. Aunt Adelina started to get messages from Denton's telegraph office down by the train depot, something that had never happened before. They were from Victor and from Willard, ordering more and more bottles of tonic. Each telegram was sent from a different place in Washington Territory and in Oregon. The twins were certainly moving around.

We were moving, too. All of us were busy making Aunt

Adelina's green wonder-worker. Uncle Silas was taking a hand, measuring out herbs and pounding roots in the mortar and helping to stir, with Xerxes working beside him. He had taken to Xerxes at once, and so had we.

Mrs. Apley's stove and kitchen were going full chisel, and Aunt Adelina rushed constantly from our Poplar Street house to the Apley's Sycamore Street house, putting in the special, most expensive herbs and, of course, her secret ingredient.

Whatever that secret was, she guarded it closely. There was a big cedar chest in her bedroom, and she always kept it locked. Her reticule was inside that, I was certain. What's more, she wore the little gold key to the chest on a chain around her neck. Thunderation, she didn't trust anybody at all!

Caralee started to warm toward me and asked me one day at recess if I wanted to borrow one of the new books that her parents had given her for her birthday.

I told her, "No, I don't. I haven't the time to read anything but the essays of Ralph Waldo Emerson these days because I'm helping my aunt in her business. She has lots of partners now, but she still needs me. She even needs Henry Frederick when she can get him away from the pigpen. Good-bye, Caralee, I have to get home now."

And then I left her, running home before she could say, "Well, I never!" or ask me any more embarrassing things about Mr. Whitlow.

As usual, Mr. Whitlow had been as right as the rain that had fallen all winter. This time the tonic was a success, and since orders were pouring in, money ought to soon follow.

It was the middle of April, and things were going better for us. Uncle Silas was home again and working. Mr. Heffer was courting Mrs. Apley, who'd made him believe the fib about her swollen scalded hand and the ruby ring under the bandage. Our house had been saved from the bank until July. We'd almost put Mr. Barlow Bradshaw, devil take him, out of our minds, and now that his debt was paid Uncle Silas had learned not to sign notes for anybody again. It even appeared that I might be enrolling in the Denton Academy in late September.

So it was almost a victory supper Aunt Adelina gave on the first day of May. It wasn't corned beef and cabbage or fern pie this time but fried chicken from our coop and trout from the Willamette, along with fresh vegetables from our garden. Aunt Adelina and Mama did the cooking on this occasion.

Naturally, Gus Heffer was invited. He came by wagon and brought over two more kegs of alcohol. He and Uncle Silas seemed friendly enough, but he and Mrs. Apley were like two turtledoves, sitting next to each other at the table. He boned her fish for her, and she cut up his chicken for him, even though her hand was bandaged.

Xerxes sat next to me and was polite as could be. He'd been introduced as Xerxes Westlake, and he said almost nothing at the table because he was scared that Mr. Heffer might ask him some questions about Pennsylvania, where the Westlakes had lived, and he had never set foot in the state.

Tonight Zenobia and Yolanda were dolled up like little

May queens because they'd just delivered May baskets to elderly ladies that afternoon. Mrs. Apley had been at the henna again and her hair blazed over her lavender-taffeta gown. She was blooming now—blooming like a red rose!

And then it happened. The bloom went right off the rose. Right there at our supper table what we had feared took place.

Xerxes was passing around the chicken gravy for the second time and asked politely, "Does anybody want some more gravy?"

Nobody said yes, and that should have told him to put the gravy boat down. But he was so danged polite that, in a moment of silence when everyone was chewing, he asked, "How about you, Mama? Don't you want more gravy? Your potatoes look dry."

I caught my breath in horror, hoping Mr. Heffer hadn't heard Xerxes's slip.

"*Mama?*" I saw Gus Heffer's fork stop on the way to his mouth. He looked first at Mrs. Apley, who had her eyes fixed on her plate, then across the table at Xerxes. "My boy, didn't I just hear you call Mrs. Apley *Mama?*"

"*Gus!*" Mrs. Apley looked up, then said again, "Oh, Gus. We wanted to tell you about Xerxes!"

"Tell me? Tell me that there are even more of you?" He got up. "Every time I come over here for a meal, you serve up another Apley." He asked Xerxes sharply, "Are you a twin, too?"

"No, sir, there's only one of me."

"That's more than enough." Heffer threw down his napkin. "Please come on out onto the veranda with me, Eleanora. I have something to say to you that I don't want to say in front of other folks." He gave Aunt Adelina and Uncle Silas each a hard look, then snorted. *"Xerxes Westlake, huh?"*

Out he stalked and out went Mrs. Apley behind him with a red-faced, flustered look.

"Oh, my," came from Mama. Then she giggled nervously.

"Amen to that, Cassie," said Uncle Silas.

"I'm sorry, everybody," said Xerxes mournfully.

"You ought to be," scolded Yolanda.

"We didn't tattle to him—not us," put in Zenobia.

I didn't say anything. Neither did Aunt Adelina nor Henry Frederick, who was staring at his trout, shaking his head.

Mrs. Apley came back alone with tearstains on her face. She sank down in her chair and said over the muffling of her handkerchief, "Gus says two Apleys are fine. Three are all right. Four is really too much, but he won't stand for five! He says he doesn't want that many children to start our marriage with. I said I'd give back the ruby ring to him just as soon as my hand is healed." She wailed, "I love Gus Heffer, but I meant what I told him."

Henry Frederick asked her, "Did he tell you straight out that he wanted the ring back?"

"Isn't the ring yours, Mama?" Yolanda wanted to know.

"I suppose it is. Gus didn't demand it back, but I want to be honorable about this. I'm crushed. Crushed. Gus says I'm a scheming female, even if I'm a one-quarter business partner of his. I'd so hoped he'd come to love Xerxes in time."

"It sure don't look that way now, does it, Ma?" asked Zenobia, who was giving her big brother a very cross look.

We needed something good to happen after that because

Mrs. Apley was stricken with a bad case of the doleful dumps. She didn't take to her bed with the vapors, but I suspected that she added a bit more salt to the tonic by shedding tears into the pots on her stove.

Uncle Silas, who visited the Payday now and then, said Mr. Heffer was adding some salt to his daily glass of beer, too.

As for me, I was too busy washing bottles and labeling them and stirring pots to take a hand in the punctured romance, but it was on my mind a lot. It appeared that even love among grown-ups, something that should be joyful, also had its bad side. Look at the troubles my uncle and aunt had gone through, and they'd been married for nearly forty years!

Willard came back to Denton on the train a couple days after the dinner party. My, but he was full of beans and news! He brought orders for more tonic and some bragging stories about how he'd made tough store owners almost beg to buy Mrs. Westlake's green wonder-worker. Nobody had suspected who Mrs. Hogg and Mr. Bohr were. In his sales talk he'd made a big thing out of what his mother had written him about how none of the Apleys or the Westlakes got la grippe the way so many folks in Denton had.

He was glad to see Xerxes, who had moved to the Apley house now that the secret was out. Willard told his mother not to fret about losing Mr. Heffer because when she was rich from the sales of the tonic, she'd have to "beat off the willing bachelors with a baseball bat." He said she'd done the right thing in pawning the ruby ring. And then he told her about his engagement. He'd renewed his acquaintance with the daughter of a druggist up in Olympia, Washington Territory, courted her, and was now betrothed. Her father had ordered lots of bottles of tonic and promised to push it to ladies as a "la grippe staver-offer and blood builder." So would his four brothers, who were also pharmacists and store-keepers in Washington.

And then Willard left Denton for the Territory once more, after promising to send a wagon down for tonic, kissing his ma good-bye, and making a quick trip to the Apley and Westlake pigsties when Henry Frederick told him, in my hearing, "Victor wanted you to take a look at the hogs when you came home."

Willard didn't leave any cash, though. He said there hadn't been time yet to show any real profit, and the money he got now mostly went for his traveling expenses.

So we went on making more tonic, using Mr. Heffer's alcohol and his empty bottles, being grateful that he didn't demand any money from us because we had none to give him.

He didn't ask for anything, as a matter of fact. He talked to Uncle Silas at the saloon but never once came near our house or the Apleys'. I supposed that was because he thought we were all "scheming females." But again I was too busy to take a hand in the failed romance.

Victor showed up ten days after Willard had left. He went directly to our pigpen, even though Henry Frederick was at the store on an errand. I sneaked out behind the hen house to see what Victor was up to, and I saw him leaning over the sty, talking to the pigs and watching them. What a grunting they had set up. Henry Frederick hadn't needed to warn me to keep away from the pigpen because the pigs had turned "ferocious." They smelled too much now that it was nearly summer for me to get any closer. And I could see why they would be ferocious, being pestered so much by Henry Frederick's constant attention.

I watched Victor until I saw him turn away from the sty. Then I ran to the house and told Aunt Adelina, "He's coming here now."

"Good, Lucinda. Pour him a cup of coffee. He must have something interesting to tell us, too."

When he'd wrapped his long legs around the rungs of one of our kitchen chairs, Victor started in on his news. "I've got orders for three hundred bottles of the elixir."

Uncle Silas told him, "That's good to hear, but we're going to have to work day and night, all of us, to fill that big an order."

Victor Apley only nodded and blew on his coffee to cool it. "Then you'll have to scout around Denton and get some other kitchens going or rent an empty building, Mr. Westlake. But that'll have to wait till the cash starts rolling in. I've brought orders this time but no cash because I need the money for traveling."

"Did you go home yet, or did you come here first?" I asked him.

"I came here. I figured it was most important. After all, it's your aunt's tonic."

"Yes, but it's your mother's and Mr. Heffer's, too."

He only nodded when I thought my information might have jolted him. "Yep, I know about the partnership."

"Do you know about the engagement and its being busted and the ruby ring being pawned?" I asked him.

"Yep. It's too bad, but Gus Heffer ain't the only fish in the sea for Ma."

"He's the only one she wants, Victor Apley!" I flared at him. He was heartless in my estimation.

He laughed at me, which proved that I was right. "I'm courting myself these days—a girl in Roseburg, one in Eugene, and another in Portland. Their papas are all ordering and selling the green wonder-worker in their stores."

I said, "Well, your brother Willard isn't running around breaking female hearts. He's engaged to be married to *one* lady."

"I know about Willard. We met in Portland last week. That's how I found out about Xerxes and your supper party and about Ma and Heffer. It seems to me that it was downright risky for you to invite Mr. Heffer over for supper."

He drank the rest of his coffee, got up from the table, shook hands with Uncle Silas, told Aunt Adelina and me to keep "stirring and bottling," and then asked Mama, "Mrs. Howard, would you ask Henry Fred to come over to Ma's house as soon as he gets back home from his errand?"

"Yes, of course, Victor."

When Victor had left, I said from the stove, "I'll bet you anything he wants to see Henry Frederick about pigs."

"They do seem to have pigs in common," said Uncle Silas. "Well, it's nice to see young people with some real interests in life. It keeps them out of trouble."

I snorted as I stirred, trying to keep the tonic from scorching on the bottom. "They've got pigs on the brain. Victor Apley even talks to them. I saw him get them to the point where they were really squealing and grunting at him. They sure sound ferocious these days."

"Well then," said Aunt Adelina, "we certainly won't go near them."

"I wonder if the railing around the pen is strong enough. I don't want Henry Frederick to get hurt by a pig," said Mama.

"Don't worry, Cassie," answered Uncle Silas. "I built that pigpen myself. It's the strongest in Denton. Those animals would have to reach the size of small elephants to break it down."

We had a breather toward the end of May, after we'd sent a wagonload of tonic bottles northward along the road that led to Portland and Washington Territory.

Now that we could rest a bit I decided to try to take a hand in the bunged-up romance that was making both Mrs. Apley and Mr. Heffer pine away. They were both losing weight and looking very down at the mouth these days. Not even a bright, sunny day could perk them up.

One Saturday afternoon I went to the back door of the Payday Saloon and gave the bell rope one hard pull.

When the bartender came out, I told him, "I don't want any gin or whiskey or beer or brandy or anything like that. But I would like to talk to Mr. Heffer. Will you please tell him that it's Lucinda Lavina Howard out here to see him?"

"Sure, little lady." And he was off.

After a spell of waiting, Mr. Heffer came out and stood scowling in the doorway of the back room, with this thumbs stuck in his vest pockets. He looked quite peaked, I thought.

I started in, "I have to speak with you on a matter of great importance."

He told me, "I never thought I would say this to a child your age, but I am wary of you, Lucinda. I'm nervous around your aunt now and even more nervous around Eleanora, although we are partners in the same business. They're both female schemers of the worst order, it seems to me. I feel that you probably are, too. I suspect that I am one unprotected man around your family and the Apleys."

So I said, "But you didn't give Xerxes a chance! He's quiet and not one bit like Victor and Willard. Ask Uncle Silas about Xerxes. He likes him. Xerxes doesn't play tricks on folks. He only said he was Xerxes Westlake because he was told to."

Heffer ignored that. "What brings you here today, Lucinda? Does your aunt know you came?" He was being sterner than he'd ever been before with me.

"No, sir, not a soul knows I'm here. I'm here because I'm sorry about what happened. I would have been over a lot sooner except that I was so busy making the elixir, which is selling splendidly. I came out of the goodness of my heart because I want you to get betrothed again to Mrs. Apley. She's pining away for you night and day. Zenobia says she cries out 'Gus, Gus!' in her sleep."

"Does she now?" He was still looking stern.

I went on, "She weeps, too. I've seen her cry when anyone speaks your name to her or when another keg of your alcohol comes in the wagon to her kitchen door."

"Eleanora weeps, huh?" he asked me thoughtfully.

"You bet she does. She cries plenty over you slipping her

the mitten, breaking the engagement. Besides, she's in terrible trouble because of the ruby ring she wants to give back to you."

"How's that? What kind of trouble, Lucinda?" He'd snapped at this all right.

I'd laid awake half of last night practicing what I was going to say to him right at this moment. "Mr. Heffer, you know that Eleanora was scalded badly when she spilled the tonic on her hand, and you know that she had the ruby ring on at the time."

"Yes, yes, I know all that."

"Well, her hand isn't healing the way it was supposed to. The finger the ruby is on is still so swelled up that you can hardly see the ring. She went to see a fancy doctor in Portland so she wouldn't have to have your ring filed off. She's trying to give it back to you in good shape in case you want to give it to some other lady someday." I took a deep sobbing breath. "And the doctor told her that if she refuses to have the ring filed off with a saw, he will have to cut off her finger. That's what she's thinking of doing to please you, Mr. Heffer, getting her finger sawed off. So I think it would be very nice of you to forgive her for concealing Xerxes, don't you?"

To my horror he was smiling. He was heartless, too. He chuckled all at once, making my blood run cold in my veins. Then he said, "Do you expect me to believe that story you just told me, Lucinda?"

I felt my face catching fire from embarrassment and wished I'd dabbed on some of my aunt's eggshell powder before I'd come here. "You don't believe it?" I asked.

"No. I don't. Oh, I believe that nobody sent you to me

today, but I don't believe one word about Eleanora's finger.
No doctor would ever do that if a ring could be filed off.
I have set eyes on Eleanora several times by accident since
your aunt's supper party. She still has the bandage on, so I
assume she did get a bad scalding. I assume, too, that my
ruby is under that bandage, which is a good safe place for the
ring."

Thinking of the Portland pawnshop, I felt I could truthfully say, "Yes, it's in a safe place, all right."

He went on, "Is Eleanora truly pining? Tell me the truth,
please, Lucinda."

I was looking right at him when I said, "Yes, sir, she truly
is pining. She suspects she's going to get rich the way the
twins keep telling her, but all the same she's pining. It
doesn't do them any good to tell her that someday soon she'll
have to beat off bachelors who want to marry her because
she's a rich widow. Gold does not mend a broken heart, you
know. Remember, too, that she's a partner of Aunt Adelina's
and of yours."

"So, Lucinda Howard, you think Mrs. Apley and I ought
to patch things up and get married and put our two one
quarters together to make a half? Is that why you think I
ought to make Mrs. Apley Mrs. Heffer—for the sake of the
tonic trade?"

"No, sir. I think you and Mrs. Apley aren't getting any
younger, and you ought to be as happy as you can as long as
you can. Besides, neither of you are very good testimonials
for the elixir right now, and I happen to know you both
take it every day. Good day to you, Mr. Heffer. I think I've
said all I plan to say." This had been tricky.

His words floated after me as I walked down the saloon alley. "I won't tell anybody in your family or the Apley family that you came here, and I won't tell them what you said to me either."

I supposed I should have called back "thank you" over my shoulder, but I was too embarrassed to do that. I'd made a fool of myself, all right. Caralee's mother had been right about the perils of matchmaking.

Halfway home I recalled what else he'd said, and I stopped in my tracks not far from the front of the Reverend Curley's parsonage. Mr. Heffer had said he wouldn't *tell* the Apleys about me. Well then, that ought to mean that he was going to start seeing Mrs. Apley again! Thunderation, how wonderful!

Mrs. Curley was just closing the gate to her front yard as I passed by. I told her, "Please tell the Reverend Curley for me that he's right when he says in church that 'the Lord works in wondrous ways his miracles to perform.'"

And then I went on, leaving her holding the gate open, staring after me.

Mr. Heffer didn't let any grass grow under his boots. He went right over to Eleanora's that same night I'd talked with him, and somehow or other the two of them got their betrothal back on the track.

Yolanda told me what happened at school Monday morning at recess. "Lucinda, Mr. Heffer came to see Ma last Saturday night, and she sent Yolanda and me up to bed right away without our Saturday-night baths."

"It was too soon to go to bed, and I was dirty," put in Zenobia.

Yolanda ignored her. "Mr. Heffer and Ma and Xerxes talked for a spell in the parlor. Then Xerxes came up to bed, and Ma and Mr. Heffer jawed some more down below."

"Yes, yes?" I asked excitedly.

"Well, they're getting hitched up together again," Yolanda said.

"What about Xerxes, though? Does Mr. Heffer take to him now?"

"I guess so. Xerxes said at breakfast, which he cooked for us because Ma wasn't out of bed yet, that Mr. Heffer's going to send him to Denton Academy because he's smart."

I hadn't expected anything quite that good, but I was pleased. "What did Xerxes do that made Heffer take to him that much?"

Zenobia explained, "Xerxes showed him his report from the school he went to up in Canada. Xerxes has never got anything but A's in his whole life. Ma can't understand it. Xerxes ain't much like Yolanda or me or Victor or Willard or—"

"Or who?" I asked, giggling. She must mean her mother.

"Like our pa, who is up in heaven. That's who." And now Yolanda grabbed her little sister by the hand and dragged her off toward the schoolhouse, leaving me still giggling to myself.

I found my aunt and Mrs. Apley happy as could be in my aunt's kitchen when I got home that afternoon.

"It's all just dandy again now, Lucinda," cried Mrs. Apley.

"I know that. Yolanda and Zenobia told me at school. When will you and Mr. Heffer be getting married?"

"Gus told me to set a date that pleased me, but naturally

I want to have my ruby ring back first. So I won't be a June bride because I doubt if I'll have the money to go to the pawnshop by then."

Aunt Adelina was smiling. "The date of a wedding is very important, you know." I saw her lean back in her chair, fold her hands in her lap, fix her eyes on the ceiling, then ask, "I wonder about July then."

She waited, and I waited, then she asked, "August, perhaps?"

We both waited while the hairs prickled on my neck again.

"September?" was the next soft question.

No anvil dropped upstairs this time. No tinkling of a teacup, no sound from the warming oven. *The house shook all over.*

"Was that an earthquake, missus?" cried Mrs. Apley, clutching at the kitchen table, where the cups were dancing.

"No, Eleanora. It was nothing at all. September will be an excellent time for you and Mr. Heffer to marry."

In the second week of June, Victor returned full of vim and vinegar and with a profit of four hundred and twenty dollars, which he handed over to Aunt Adelina. It was up to her as the half owner to divide it. Victor had more than money with him. He had testimonials about how good the tonic was from six different people—the three girls he was courting in various Oregon cities and their mothers.

I heard Uncle Silas muttering under his breath, after Victor and Henry Frederick had gone out to see the pigs, "I wonder if those are testimonials to Adelina's elixir or to Victor's courting?"

I didn't know, so I said nothing. That talk I had with Mr. Heffer behind the Payday had been a lesson to me, all right, about meddling in matters of romance. I didn't intend to talk about Victor Apley's trifling with the affections of druggists' daughters.

Aunt Adelina didn't have a supper party for the Apleys and Mr. Heffer, but she did have Mrs. Apley and Victor and Xerxes over for tea before Victor left town again.

"Where do you plan to go this time, my boy?" Uncle Silas asked Victor.

Victor said, as he shoved pound cake baked especially for the occasion into his mouth, "I'm headed down to California this time, traveling mostly by stagecoach, which isn't so comfortable. I plan to make my headquarters in Frisco." All at once he turned his head to look at Uncle Silas. "What's the name of the galoot who got you to sign that debt for him at the bank? I mean the one who ran out on you on New Year's Day?"

"His name is Bradshaw, Barlow Bradshaw."

"So, that's the right name, huh?" Victor looked at his mother. "Ma, you said it was Baxter Bradford."

"Victor, I don't truly know the crooked galoot," said Mrs. Apley.

"No matter, Ma. I got the name straight now. Mr. West-lake, isn't that man supposed to be somewhere down in California?"

"That's where he told Zenobia he was going on New Year's Day," agreed my aunt.

"Well, Mrs. Westlake, I think maybe I'll keep my eyes

peeled for gents by the name of Bradshaw, and if I happen to run into this one, I plan to tell him a thing or two."

Uncle Silas warned, "There's no use doing that, Victor. The debt's been paid, thanks to your mother's generosity. My deal with Bradshaw was perfectly legal, unfortunately. You couldn't set the police on him, even if he was still here in the state of Oregon."

"That's not what I plan to do. If I run into him, I'm going to tell him that the formula he gave Mrs. Westlake is turning out to be a gold mine, as well as a real true-blue wonderworker. Then I'll say 'Ha, ha!' for all of you right in his face."

Aunt Adelina said quietly, as she put her teacup down next to the stereopticon viewer, "Don't bother with Mr. Bradshaw, Victor. He no longer matters in our lives. I don't think that the Tuscarora Tonic really concerns him anymore."

"Why doesn't it, Mrs. Westlake?"

She told him, "Because it isn't his tonic now. His debt to the bank has been paid by my husband. The formula is mine, my weeds from the wilderness."

I caught her swift smile at me, one that disappeared almost at once. Yes, I thought I understood what she meant, even if he didn't. She'd made a lot of changes in the Tuscarora Tonic, but because Victor had been so curious about it at first she wasn't going to come out and tell him that.

"Well, all I got to say is that you better take care of that formula of yours," answered Victor. "It's valuable now. You guard that well, Mrs. Westlake."

"I shall do that, Victor. It's in a safe place."

Afterward we talked about the sunny weather and about the bad shape the nation was in, according to the *Oregonian*, because of what folks called the Panic of 1873. And then we talked some about California, where Victor was bound next and where Uncle Silas had visited years ago.

That night I came down secretly to the parlor with a candle and hauled out the big Bible and opened it. Yes, sir, just as I had thought. There, stuck in the middle of the Book of Ezekiel, was the Tuscarora Tonic formula on top of Aunt Adelina's and Uncle Silas's wedding certificate.

Shaking my head, I shut the Bible and went back up to bed. I could think of better, safer places than that one.

I surely hoped Aunt Adelina knew what she was doing.

CHAPTER X

"He's Got It, Silas!"

Willard came back to town before Victor did. This time he not only brought the great big sum of five hundred dollars and more orders for Aunt Adelina's tonic but also a photograph of his betrothed up in Washington Territory. I thought she appeared to be a bit popeyed, but that could be because she was being courted by Willard Apley. Deep down I suspected Victor's three Oregon girls were also abnormally popeyed. The Apley twins were surely whirlwinds in trousers. You never knew what they were going to say or do next. Every time they were around me I felt ready to jump out of my skin and knew that if I was being courted by one of them I'd be popeyed with expectation, too.

Willard was just full of instructions—or rather commands

—to Aunt Adelina and Uncle Silas. What he ordered them to do really came down to one thing: make more bottles of tonic. "Work harder, get more kitchens going, get more workers, get more herbs. Get the orders I send down to you filled fast and on their way."

Then after a quick trip to the pigpens and the Apley house, Willard got back on the train to Washington Territory to revisit his betrothed's uncles, who had bought the green wonder-worker.

We all saw him off at the train station. Mr. Heffer had been positively beaming as he waved to Willard, with one arm around Mrs. Apley's waist and his hand on Xerxes's shoulder. Part of the smile on Heffer's face may have come from the fact that Aunt Adelina had finally given him some cash from the money that Willard had brought back. Mr. Heffer had surely been a patient man about waiting for his profit, and he'd never failed to send over the alcohol for the tonic's solvent, even when he was mad as a boiled snake at Mrs. Apley, Xerxes, and Aunt Adelina.

Because the day after Willard departed was a Saturday I got to go up to Portland again on the train with Aunt Adelina and Mrs. Apley.

Their first call was at the pawnshop. Again I had to wait out on the boardwalk because pawnshops weren't proper places for people my age, but by pressing my nose against the window I could see beyond the iron grating. I watched the little pawnbroker take the lapel watch down off a hook on the wall on the right side of him and then unlock a drawer behind him on the wall and take something out of it. Aha—the ruby ring!

The ladies didn't waste any time at the pawnbroker's after they'd redeemed the watch and ring. They came sailing out before I had time to wipe away the smudge my nose had made on the window. I noticed that Aunt Adelina was wearing her watch on her bosom, and Mrs. Apley must have left the bandage she'd worn in the pawnbroker's wastebasket. Once more the ring sparkled on her finger.

Afterward, we all walked to the big pharmacy on Second Street and then down to the little one on Jefferson. Outside of the second one, Aunt Adelina told us, "My dears, I must ask you once more to stay out here while I buy the item I need. Why not go to the milliner's shop next door and admire the bonnets in the window?"

Mrs. Apley and I did, and we did more than admire them. We went inside, and she bought a woven-straw bonnet with marigolds, violets, and cornflowers on the top and a deep-green velvet ribbon streaming down the back. Naturally, she wore it home. It was quite startling on top of her red hair, so much so that people turned to look at us as we walked back toward the depot. I was quite sure that these Portlanders had never seen such elegance before, and I was proud to be with Mrs. Apley, as we walked along with our bags of herbs, roots, and, of course, the secret ingredient in my aunt's little black reticule.

Well, one thing was certain. We weren't ruined anymore.

Throughout the month of June we made tonic and more tonic, and after school had been dismissed for the summer in the second week of the month, I worked my fingers to the bone. Orders from Victor and Willard kept flooding in by telegram and letter. Uncle Silas hired two Denton ladies, who lived near our house on Poplar Street, to help make the tonic, so Aunt Adelina was kept very busy going to their houses and the Apley house to add the herbs and the secret ingredient. I went with her sometimes, though I always had to leave the kitchens when it came time to open her reticule for the secret thing. She was the only one who truly knew all that went into the green wonder-worker!

The first day of July, a most astonishing thing happened, and it was all Victor Apley's fault. He hadn't paid one bit of attention to what Aunt Adelina and Uncle Silas had told him at their tea party before he went down to San Francisco. He'd found Mr. Barlow Bradshaw and told him about how successful the tonic was, just as he'd threatened.

On that day I went from the kitchen, where I was working, to answer the front doorbell, expecting perhaps the Reverend Curley, who was taking a mysterious interest in me all at once. Instead, I was astounded to find Mr. Barlow Bradshaw standing out on the veranda. He was as big as life and very unwelcome.

"*You?*" was the one word that burst out of me. Before I could shut the door in his whiskers, Mama was there behind me. "Who is that, Lucinda? The Reverend Curley again?"

I hissed at her, "No, it's the devil."

He didn't hear me, but she did. She took one look at him and pressed her hand to her bosom and said, "Oh!"

Bradshaw's teeth flashed in his ginger-colored beard. "Is Mr. Westlake at home today?"

"Yes." I saw Mama's hand on the banisters go white as she hesitated. Seeing Bradshaw a couple of months ago would have given her a fright, but now I suspected she was just trying to keep a grip on her temper. She said after a time, "Come into the parlor, Mr. Bradshaw."

I wanted to add, ". . . said the spider to the fly," but decided not to.

"Lucinda," Mama ordered me, "please go get your uncle."

I turned around and went out to the kitchen, where Aunt Adelina and Uncle Silas were pounding herbs and roots. "Mama has just let Mr. Barlow Bradshaw into the house," I told them. "He's in the parlor now. He wants to see you, Uncle Silas."

My aunt sighed. "Oh, dear, I think I sense the fine hand of Victor Apley in this, Silas."

He said sourly, "More than likely, blast that pup. Well, let's go see Bradshaw and find out what he wants."

"Silas, please don't sign any more things for him."

"Have no fear, Adelina." After taking off the long butcher's apron he wore to protect his clothes, he paused at the kitchen door to say, "Adelina, you get out of that apron, too, and come with me to the parlor. Hell's bells, it's your tonic! Hadn't you planned to come out and see Bradshaw?"

I saw her flash a smile at him. "Yes, I had planned to come, Silas, but you don't know how pleased I am to have you ask me. His business was with you in the first place, not with me. I didn't enter into it until you gave me the formula for the Tuscarora Tonic."

"No, Adelina, Bradshaw cogged me and doing that hurt you and your sister's family. Don't think I'll be forgetting that. I wonder what he wants now?"

"Well, Silas, let's go to the parlor and find out together."

I came right along behind them because I wanted to know what brought Mr. Bradshaw to Denton all the way from California.

He was sitting on the settee and Mama sat across from him glaring when we all trooped in.

Before either my uncle or aunt could say anything, Bradshaw jumped up and said, "By golly, it's fine to see you again, Silas, my friend." He came forward to grab my uncle's hand and pumped it up and down until Uncle Silas finally wiggled it free, which wasn't too easy to do.

Then my uncle asked coldly, "What brings you back up to these parts, Bradshaw?"

"Why, Silas, I've done well in business down in Frisco. I came up here as quick as I could to pay back that three-hundred-dollar debt you took on for me last year."

Uncle Silas's voice was even chillier as he said, "That came due the end of March, and I paid off the bank. It's July now, Barlow."

"Did that debt to Banker Lambertson fall due that soon?" Bradshaw pretended to be surprised, but nobody was taken in by his acting.

Uncle Silas said, "No, Barlow, you wouldn't forget a thing like that—not an important man in business like you."

"Well, I did this time, Silas." Bradshaw chuckled. "Anyhow I brought you that remaining two hundred and fifty-two dollars, and here it is right now." He took a brown envelope out from the inside of his pearl-gray coat.

Another brown envelope! I looked at it, then at him, and tried to put a sneer on my face the way actors did on the stage in melodramas that had come to Denton.

I watched Uncle Silas take the envelope, open it, and pull out a number of greenbacks.

"There's the full amount there, Silas," Bradshaw said. "So now, if you please, I'd like you to return the formula for that Indian herb tonic I gave you last January."

Aunt Adelina spoke up. "It isn't his to give, Mr. Bradshaw. He signed it over to me that very day."

"*To you?*" Bradshaw looked astonished.

"Yes, to me. Didn't Victor Apley tell you that when you spoke with him down in San Francisco?"

"I don't know who you're talking about, Mrs. Westlake."

"But we think you do, Mr. Bradshaw," I said, even if I was talking out of turn. "Victor Apley must have told you how well we were all doing making the tonic."

Mr. Bradshaw stopped telling lies. He said, "All right, I saw a young man named Apley down there. The formula you have belongs to me now that I've paid back that money due on the loan."

"No, it belongs to me," came from Aunt Adelina calmly. "However, if you want to have it back, you can dicker with me, I suppose."

"Dicker with *her*, Silas?" Bradshaw was staring at my uncle and getting red in what I could see of his face under his whiskers.

"It's her formula, Barlow, and it's her tonic," explained Uncle Silas.

Bradshaw swung around to face my aunt. "All right, madam, how am I to dicker with you?"

She told him, "You could start by offering me a fair price for it—something around five hundred dollars to start with."

"Madam, that formula is mine! Hand it over, please. I won't pay a nickel for what is rightfully mine."

I saw her turn to Uncle Silas and say in a very sweet voice that sent chills up and down my back, "Silas, would you consider returning Mr. Bradshaw's money to him? If you do that, I will have clear and free ownership of the Tuscarora Tonic formula."

Thunderation, what was going on around here?

I watched Uncle Silas turn to Bradshaw and hold out the envelope of money. "Here, Bradshaw, here's your cash. Adelina and I don't want it. We don't need it anymore."

"Silas, I'll get the law and sheriff on the two of you," said Bradshaw, grabbing the envelope.

Aunt Adelina told him, "I doubt very much if there's any law anywhere that says anyone has to accept money forced on him by another person. That would be like robbery in reverse. We have the impression, Mr. Bradshaw, that you are interested in the Tuscarora Tonic because you're aware now that I am making money from it. I will not give it up to you. My price still starts at five hundred dollars."

"And I won't pay that, madam."

"I doubt very much if you could," Mama put in all at once, looking up from the doily she had been crocheting.

I said, "I agree with Mama. I don't think you've done so danged well down in California as you say you have. If you had, you wouldn't have made tracks up here so fast once Victor Apley bragged to you."

"I don't have to listen to words of folly from children like this little girl here." Bradshaw jammed his hat onto his head and went out of the parlor so fast the portieres blew apart.

He jerked the front door open, slammed it shut, and bolted over the veranda, down the boardwalk, and out onto Poplar Street.

Mama said in an extremely calm manner, "You know, it appears to me that Victor Apley is a better salesman that we'd thought. He certainly sold Mr. Bradshaw on the idea of coming all the way back up here."

I told them all, "Mama, I don't think Victor meant to do that. All he had in mind was to get some revenge for us."

"Getting revenge can be dangerous sometimes," replied Uncle Silas.

"What do you mean?" asked Aunt Adelina.

"Adelina, I know something of Barlow Bradshaw's character. He isn't a man who likes to be turned down by anyone, let alone by a woman. And he hates to be made a fool of. I hope he goes back down to California at once."

I said, "Well, it'll be easy for us to find out. School's out for summer, so we can post Zenobia, who knows Bradshaw by sight, on the front porch of the Denton Hotel where the stagecoach leaves from. The coach leaves on Monday, Wednesday, and Friday morning, so she'll only have to sit on the hotel steps then."

"A most excellent idea, Lucinda!" answered Aunt Adelina, nodding. Then she said, "I think Denton Academy will be lucky to have you in September. You're becoming a quick and adult thinker."

I smiled with pleasure. My smile faded as I remembered some of the not-so-very-adult things I'd done this year. Tattling about Aunt Adelina's lapel watch was one. And it was a good thing, too, that Mr. Heffer hadn't told anyone about my story of Mrs. Apley's possibly getting her finger sawed off to please him. That had been very nice of him. We'd all changed our views about saloonkeepers now that we'd gotten to know Gus Heffer, who was a very fine gentleman—every bit as fine as Uncle Silas had claimed he was.

Two days later Zenobia gave us the good news that Mr. Bradshaw had boarded the southbound stage for California, and that evening her brother Victor came back on the northbound one. They had passed like ships in the night.

Victor came to our house first, bringing more money and orders for the tonic. He'd been in fine fettle, as usual, and told us that he was courting two girls in California whose papas owned mercantile stores, as well as the three girls in Oregon. I thought this was even more dreadful of him.

Uncle Silas asked him before he went to see his mother, "Victor, did you talk not long ago to a Mr. Barlow Bradshaw down in Frisco?"

"You bet I did. I told him what I said I was going to tell him. It was a real pleasure."

I said angrily, "Well, thanks to your being so smart, Mr. Bradshaw came up here to pay Uncle Silas the money he owed him, but that wasn't the real reason he called on us."

Victor asked my aunt, "What was that?"

"To demand that I return the formula for the Tuscarora Tonic."

"Did you do that?" I saw how Victor's grin disappeared. His whole face grew dark.

"No, of course not. We refused to take his money. He left before Silas ordered him out of the house, and now he's returned to California. Zenobia saw him go off today on the stagecoach."

"All the same, you'd better put that formula in the big safe at the Denton Bank, Mrs. Westlake," Victor warned.

"It's in a safe place, Victor. I'm not one bit worried about it."

"Well, I sure hope it is, Mrs. Westlake. I've met a man or two like Bradshaw since I've been traveling. He's the kind who's been just one step ahead of the sheriff, and now that times are hard I think he might not care about keeping one step ahead anymore. I'm glad to hear that he's left Denton."

"I am not afraid of Mr. Bradshaw or of anyone else, Victor," came from Aunt Adelina.

And then Victor went home, and I helped my aunt get the herbs sorted out for tomorrow's pounding and smashing and boiling. She could tell them apart just by looking at them and sniffing—but not me. They all looked pretty dried up and awful to my way of thinking. I guess I wasn't any herb woman!

I asked, "Do you trust the Apley twins, Aunt Adelina?"

"I have to, Lucinda. I need them. I have to trust them, as well as Mrs. Apley and Mr. Heffer and Silas and you—everybody who helps me to make and sell the elixir."

"But Mrs. Apley's schemed so much about her sons, and her girls don't tattle the way most little kids do. They keep things back. I'll bet you anything that they're holding back a secret or two right now."

She sighed. "Eleanora has been forced to do that sort of thing, Lucinda. She has suffered a great deal and worked very hard to keep her girls with her. She deserves some happiness now. I'm pleased that I could help her and have her help me. And tomorrow night she wants us all over at her house to share the whipped-cream cake she's making in honor of Xerxes's birthday."

Whipped-cream cake was a kind that I liked. I asked, "Will Victor still be in town then?"

"Yes, he told Henry Frederick out at the pigpen that he'll be here for three days this time."

I asked, "What are they doing out there all the time with the pigs?"

"I have no real idea. I've left the pigs to your brother and the hen house to you. Both your mother and I are far too busy to tend the pigs nowadays. I asked your brother why he has taken such a sudden interest in these pigs, and he said he liked to see them bulk up. He said that Victor believes that first tonic I made was having an interesting effect on the pigs. Henry Frederick pours a little of it on their swill each day. He says they simply dote on their victuals. Perhaps you can talk to him and Victor about the pigs at Xerxes's birthday party."

"No, ma'am. Not me—not pigs! I'll talk to Xerxes."

She eyed me sharply. "And, Lucinda, I don't think you should criticize Mrs. Apley for scheming about her boys. I seem to recall the pawning of her ruby ring as being somebody else's idea—not hers."

I said, "Yes, I know." It was a lesson to me.

We all went together to the Apley party and gorged ourselves on cake and lemonade, and the grown-ups had a wine punch supplied by Mr. Heffer. We Howards and Westlakes gave Xerxes a copy of the works of Henry David Thoreau, now that he was through with Ralph Waldo Emerson. We weren't eating fern pie or dried lentils and beans anymore, thanks to the money the green wonder-worker was making. Nowadays we could even give people birthday presents.

Uncle Silas made the toast this time. He got up in the Apley parlor and, after toasting Xerxes, said, "Here's to Adelina's elixir. I said at first that it appeared to be only 'weeds from the wilderness,' but it's turning into a fountain of pure gold. Thanks to the tonic, I paid off the money I owed to the Denton Bank this morning—a whole week early."

"To the tonic!" cried Victor. "Here's to the Tuscarora Tonic and to the downfall of old Mr. Barlow Bradshaw."

I was a bit put out. I'd had some dandelion wine on New Year's Eve, but because Xerxes, who was older than I, was only allowed to drink lemonade, I didn't get any of the wine punch. In my estimation Victor tippled too much of it.

So I said, "That isn't a very nice thing to say, Victor, wishing for somebody's downfall. He may be an almost ruined man, you know."

"Maybe he's on the brink of it, Lucy, but his kind don't get ruined easy."

"My name is *Lucinda!*" There he went again, teasing me.

"Her name *is* Lucinda," came from Mama, who must not have forgiven him for calling her the "weak sister."

"All right, Lucinda, but don't you folks go underestimating the worth of that tonic or underestimating Mr. Bradshaw. If I had to do it all over again, I wouldn't have mentioned the tonic and how successful it is to that old galoot."

We went home about ten o'clock, strolling along under the trees that lined the streets. Denton was a pretty town, and the stretch of the Willamette that went through it was smooth and wide. The clear summer night was glittering with beautiful, bright stars because there was no moon in the sky.

Uncle Silas was first to the front door to unlock it. All at once he cried out to the rest of us behind him on the veranda, "The door's wide open. I know I locked it. Henry Frederick, you go around to the back of the house."

I ran along the side of the house with my brother, and just as we got up onto the back porch a man came running out of the kitchen door, knocking Henry Frederick off his feet. I didn't see his face because of the dark and because he had his head down. He was a big man, though, with a thick body and long legs.

"Uncle Silas," I screeched, as the man ran past the hen house toward the pigsty.

Uncle Silas was there faster than I would have believed he could move. He picked my brother up off the bottom step and asked if he was hurt.

"No, I'm all right."

"Did you know who it was?"

"No, sir."

"How about you, Lucinda?"

"No, sir. I didn't see his face. He was big and fast, though. I think he ran down the alley and past the pigpen."

"All right, I'll go take a look!"

Uncle Silas hurried toward the alley as Aunt Adelina and Mama showed up. "Thank heavens, I'm wearing my lapel watch," said my aunt. "This is a robbery, I'm sure. Well, let's go inside and light the lamps and see what's been done to our house."

"Adelina, wait for Silas," warned Mama. "There could be other men in there lurking."

"No, I greatly doubt it," answered Aunt Adelina. "I think I know what has happened here. There have been some warnings—not only Victor's, but one from Mr. Whitlow and others from my Indian and ancient Egyptian spirits."

My brother said, "I want to go see how my pigs are. Then I'll come in and see if anything got stolen." And he was off.

We followed Aunt Adelina inside to the kitchen, where she lit a candle and then the wick of the lamp on the sink next to the kitchen pump. "Come on, my dears, let's go to the parlor." She called over her shoulder to Uncle Silas, who was back by now, "You didn't catch him, Silas?"

"No, he got clear away. He must be able to run like a rabbit."

"Well, let's see if he got away with what I think he came for."

The kitchen had been as we'd left it earlier that night. The drawers of the dining-room sideboard, though, were all standing open, and the paintings were down off the walls with their backs ripped off. The parlor was a real mess. The chairs and tables had been turned over, and the cushions scattered, and the paintings down here, too. The two vases that had stood on the mantel had been smashed into the fireplace. The top of the cottage organ was open so that the robber could look inside it. The books in the bookcase were lying open on top of each other, all over the carpet. The big Westlake Bible was open to the chapter of Ezekiel, alas! By peering over my aunt's shoulder I could see that marriage certificate—but that was all.

The formula was gone!

"He's got it, Silas!" said Aunt Adelina. "Bradshaw's formula for the Tuscarora Tonic is missing, and I'm sure that will be all that has been taken in the house. This isn't any run-of-the-mill robbery."

How calm she was! I marveled at her. She was a wonder.

"You think Bradshaw is behind this, Adelina?" asked Uncle Silas.

"Well, of course. He didn't come here in person. But he sent someone else, somebody he had hired and paid handsomely, I suspect. The Bible was a logical place for me to keep the formula. Bradshaw must have guessed it, or more than likely the robber must have done this sort of thing before and knew where to look."

"But, Aunt Adelina, what about the secret ingredient? Did the robber get that, too?"

My aunt came to me with the lamp in her hand, stepping over the books. She caught me to her and hugged me, saying, "Oh, my dear Lucinda, you do worry, don't you?"

I cried out, "Of course, I do! I'll bet that robber was upstairs, too."

I twisted away from her, grabbing her lamp, and ran out of the parlor and up the steps to look in the bedrooms. Yes, he'd been there. My room was a mess. So was Mama's, and my brother's was even more of one than usual. But the big bedroom my uncle and aunt shared looked as if a storm had struck it. The bedclothes were all over the floor, the bureau drawers were open, the cedar-chest lock had been smashed off, all of the winter clothes inside it were strewn over the rug.

I ran downstairs again, shouting, "He was up there, all right! He was looking for something upstairs, too. And I bet he got it!" I wailed, "Oh, what are we going to do now?"

This time I expected Aunt Adelina to cry out in alarm, but to my astonishment she began to laugh and swing her little beaded reticule, which was hanging from her wrist.

"Lucinda, he didn't get what he was looking for. I took my secret ingredient visiting with me. And, my dears, it doesn't matter one bit to me that Mr. Bradshaw hired a criminal to rob the house and carry the formula down to California. Bradshaw will think he has the formula for my elixir. He can brew the Tuscarora Tonic and set it up to compete with mine. But he will find he is very, very wrong if he thinks he has *my* wonder-working formula. Let him try to make my green one. I meant what I said when I told him I'd sell his formula back to him. His formula is not the right one."

"Then if it's not the one for the green tonic, where do you keep it?" asked Henry Frederick.

She chuckled as she put her reticule down on the table next to the lamp somebody had lit while I was upstairs. She pointed to her head. "It's here—up in here."

"Is that a safe place?" I asked her.

All at once she gave me a queer look and stopped laughing. "That was a very wise question you just asked, Lucinda. No, I don't think it is such a good place. I might fall ill someday, so I'd better do something about this situation. But right now we'll lock the house from the inside and straighten up and go to bed. I'm sure your uncle plans to go to the sheriff in the morning, but I see no reason for him to go tonight. I am positive that the only thing that will be found missing is the formula that was in the Bible."

Uncle Silas nodded at her. "By now I'm sure that a rider on a fast horse is on his way to Frisco with it." He laughed, too.

The next morning after he'd seen the sheriff, Uncle Silas and I started a new batch of the elixir in our kitchen, but Aunt Adelina didn't come downstairs at all.

When I asked Uncle Silas about her, he told me, "She's busy up there, Lucinda, doing something secret even from me. She's told your brother to go ask Mrs. Apley and Gus Heffer to come over here at eight o'clock tonight. There's to be a meeting of partners."

I said, "So that's where Henry Frederick's gone to? He isn't at the pigpen then?"

Late that July night the five grown-ups sat down together in our straightened-up parlor, and by special invitation I was there also.

"I would rather have you in here, Lucinda, than see your toes peeping from behind the portieres again," said my aunt, causing me to blush.

After we'd all had coffee, Aunt Adelina stood up and said, "You all know about the robbery from Henry Frederick, and because of it I've done something today to make sure that it will never happen again. I have written down the formula for the green tonic I make now. This is the formula I carry in my head." She held up a finger to stop their murmuring to each other. "But it isn't written down quite as you may think. I have one paper here for you, Eleanora, and another for you, Gus, and one for my sister, Cassie, and another for Silas here. In order to make the formula properly, in case I should not always be around, you will have to work together as a foursome to get the proper results."

"Adelina Pinkerton Westlake!" exploded Uncle Silas.

She went on, "You'll always have to remain good friends and partners. I suspect you will all be wise enough to keep your papers, which are quite different from each other, in well-guarded, safe places."

Mrs. Apley asked, "But what about the special secret thing? Whose paper has that been written down on?"

My aunt smiled at her friend. "No paper, Eleanora. I do not intend to tell anyone that until the time is ripe."

"Thunderation, Adelina!" Uncle Silas had come out with my very favorite word, but I couldn't tell if he was shocked by her boldness in business or if he was admiring the way her mind worked.

CHAPTER XI

"Zeenie?"

I was still marveling at what Aunt Adelina had done to protect the tonic's formula when she said that she had it in mind to go up to Portland again for more roots and herbs and, I supposed, more of the secret ingredient. Naturally, I asked to go. And so did Mrs. Apley when she was told. I wanted to go for the fast train ride and to get a peek into that little pharmacy on Jefferson Street, though I didn't tell this secret wish to anybody. Mrs. Apley wanted to go up because she needed to buy cloth for her wedding dress and for the rest of her trousseau. A dressmaker in Denton would make up the gowns for her. She was much too busy cooking up the green wonder-worker to do any sewing these days.

By now we'd changed our ways a lot, all right. We ate

meat again from the butcher shop, and we purchased books and bought new sheet-music albums for Mama to play on the cottage organ. Now and then, when the top of our stove was too filled with pots of tonic to get even a teakettle on it, Uncle Silas anounced that it was high time for all of us to eat out. We went to the Denton Hotel and sat in the dining room like travelers.

So when Mrs. Apley suggested on the train to Portland that we stay with her overnight at the biggest and best hotel in town, Aunt Adelina agreed. A hotel. How thrilling! I had never slept in one. My aunt sent her very first telegram to Uncle Silas, telling him that we'd come back on the train tomorrow.

While Mrs. Apley went shopping by herself for cloth and trimmings, my aunt and I wandered around Portland, looking into store windows. I guessed what she was looking for though she didn't say so to me—bottles of Mrs. Westlake's Wonder-Working Elixir. And thunderation, she certainly found them. I counted nine pharmacies and general stores that had displays of the bottles with her face on the label. One store had a fancy black-and-gold placard set beside a whole pyramid of bottles on glass shelves. It read:

A New Oregon Miracle—the Westlake Tonic
Pure Ingredients—Pure Power—Pure Health
Herbs and Grasses
from Oregon's Own Forest Wilderness

"My, my!" said my aunt in a very satisfied way. "I wonder who made up that sign—Victor or Willard?"

I told her, "Willard, I bet. He's the artistic one who drew

your portrait. I bet he hand-lettered it, too. Are you going inside the store and tell them that you're the lady on the bottle? You didn't go into any of the other stores here."

"No, Lucinda, I thought about it in my earlier excitement, but I have decided not to. It wouldn't be modest of me. What's more to the point, the owner might not take to me personally, and that wouldn't be good for sales."

I laughed and said, "I bet if you did go inside, the pharmacist would ask you what you put in the elixir."

"Probably, Lucinda. I don't want to risk that either. But if he did ask or if anyone ever asks, I plan to say just these words and I would like you to remember them. They came from Silas first, remember. Say, 'Oh, just some weeds from the wilderness.'"

We went next to the pharmacy on Second Street, where there were more bottles in the window and on the counter. This is where I learned just how modest my amazing Aunt Adelina was.

A young clerk stared hard at her, then at the label on the tonic bottle at his elbow, and asked, "Are you who I think you are?"

"No, young man, I am not." And that stopped him from asking any more questions while she bought more herbs and roots. But I couldn't help noticing how the other clerks stared at us after the first one had whispered to them. I wasn't sure whether I liked being famous or not. In a way it was nice having people interested in you, but not when they stared and pointed.

The little pharmacy on Jefferson Street didn't have any of the elixir in the window, more than likely because the window was only big enough to hold one huge jar of deep-purple water.

Putting my nose to the window, I peered through the purple water to see what Aunt Adelina was doing. I couldn't see anything but her shadow moving about. Hard as I looked, I couldn't see her handing anything to anyone or anyone handing anything to her. And she was out in a minute again, snapping her reticule shut. It seemed to me that she hadn't been in there long enough to say "good day, sir" to the pharmacy clerk and have him say "good day" to her. What was she buying in there so fast?

Aunt Adelina and Mrs. Apley were in good fettle that night in the dining room of the Saint Charles Hotel, which was all red plush and gold trim. They laughed over the music of violin players about Mr. Bradshaw and the Tuscarora Tonic, and then they chatted about the wedding-gown silk and other cloth Mrs. Apley had bought for her trousseau and about all the shopwindows that had had the tonic bottles in them. Mrs. Apley had also noticed them. She had even counted the numbers of bottles here and there.

After we'd eaten a dessert of cherry ice cream and pushed back our chairs to let our full stomachs be more comfortable, Mrs. Apley said, "Oh, missus, my heart would be full to the brim and running over, if it wasn't for the one sad and mournful thing still left in my life."

All at once I felt a chill creeping over me as if a window had suddenly been opened nearby.

"What would that be, Eleanora?" I noticed that my aunt had stopped smiling.

"It's my little Zeenie. I wish I could have that dear one up in Denton with me."

"Who is Zeenie, Eleanora?" asked my aunt.

"I just told you—my dear one."

"Where is he, Eleanora?"

"Down in Grass Valley, California, living with my Abner's youngest sister. But *he's* a *she*. Victor went to visit Zeenie last month, and she's just fine, though naturally she misses her ma and little sisters."

"Oh, Eleanora, *not another one!*" Aunt Adelina was as dismayed to hear this as I was.

"How old is she?" I asked Mrs. Apley.

"Eleven. She's almost twelve. She's my big girl. I wanted to keep her with me along with Yolanda and Zenobia, but I just couldn't, so when Abner's sister said she'd take her, I agreed. How my dear Abner did dote on Zeenie!"

I counted on my fingers now. "Well, it appears to me that you've got Victor and Willard and Xerxes and Yolanda and Zenobia and Zeenie. That makes two Z's you have. Did Mr. Apley like the letter Z?"

"No, that wasn't his favorite letter, Lucinda, and it ain't true that there are two Z's." Mrs. Apley was looking very proud. "My girl's name is spelled with an X! I got two X's, not two Z's. Abner fancied the letter X. The girl's name is Xenia—*X-e-n-i-a*. Xenia was the name of Abner's grandma, you see."

My aunt asked with a strange look on her face, "Eleanora, what is the girl's middle name?"

I said, "Thunderation, does she have one?"

"Of course, Lucinda. It's *X-a-n-t-h-i-p-p-e*. That was an old-time Greek lady, according to what somebody told Abner when we was in the market for a middle name."

Aunt Adelina muttered, "Yes, that was the name of the wife of Socrates, the philosopher who lived over two thousand years ago, come to think about it."

I was impressed. They did come up with two X names for their girl, even if they had to reach back a long ways for the middle one.

Aunt Adelina asked next, "Eleanora, have you told Gus about Xenia yet?"

"Not yet." She shook her red head. "I'm sort of scared to since he carried on so about Xerxes." She turned to my aunt, "But I want so to have my girl with me at my wedding in September. Couldn't she come to your house and bunk there and claim to be a Howard the way Xerxes claimed to be a Westlake?"

"Eleanora, what does she look like? Could she pass for a Howard? Does she look like Xerxes?"

"Yep, she could. She doesn't resemble him at all. She's yellow-haired like the other girls."

My aunt said, "Well, I can surely understand your wanting to have your family all together at your wedding. So, yes, I suppose you may bring Xenia to our home." Aunt Adelina crumpled her napkin into a ball beside her plate. "Let her come late in August. That should give me time to prepare everyone for her arrival."

"Oh, thank you, missus, you are the kindest, nicest lady in the whole wide world."

My aunt ignored that flattery. She said, "Now, Eleanora, let's get one thing settled about this for certain. When do you plan to introduce Xenia to Mr. Heffer?"

"When the time is ripe."

"But it may never seem ripe to you, Eleanora. Please bear in mind that you cannot spring Xenia on Mr. Heffer after you're married to him. It wouldn't be fair to Gus."

"All right, I'll set my mind to working as to how to tell Gus. Maybe Xerxes will help. He hasn't seen his sister in years. There's a lot of miles between Canada and California, you know."

"We do know that, Eleanora," said Aunt Adelina.

Mama was shocked and Uncle Silas mad to hear about Xenia, but they gave in to Aunt Adelina when they heard that Mrs. Apley had promised that Gus would be told the truth before the wedding.

Henry Frederick let me know that he hoped Xenia would "take to pigs" better than Xerxes, if he had to live under the same roof with her for a time. Otherwise, he didn't care one way or another. After all, she'd be sharing my room, and I'd have to keep her company, not him.

His harping about pigs all the time made me ask him finally, "What are you doing out there? Are you riding those pigs, or are you currycombing them?"

He gave me a very suspicious and sharp-eyed look and said, "No. They aren't horses, you know."

Our two sows littered the first and second weeks in August, so Henry Frederick practically lived at the sty. He seemed very excited about the piglets and kept looking every day for Victor to reappear. Willard came briefly with more orders and cash, but Victor was the one that Henry Frederick seemed to be waiting for.

We heard from Victor at a distance that second week in

August. He sent cash by the stagecoach company and judging from the big amount, either the courting of the storekeepers' daughters was booming or the sales of the tonic were. He also sent a very queer letter addressed to Henry Frederick, which my brother showed to all of us.

It said, "Whatever you do, Henry Fred, don't you let anybody in your family or in my family kill any of the pigs for their pork. Don't let anybody touch a hair of their heads! You guard those beasts with your life. And if the piglets have been born, you keep an eye on them night and day."

I said, "My, but he does give orders to you, doesn't he?"

My brother said, "He has a right to. We are friends."

Uncle Silas asked him, as he came to supper, "What is the matter, boy? Is the pork poisoned? Is that the effect of the first elixir your aunt made, to poison the meat just when I've got my taster set for pork chops?"

Henry Frederick scowled at all of us over the supper table and said, "I intend to guard them with my life, all right. Keep away. Don't you dare upset the sows. They might roll on the piglets and kill them. Victor said you'll learn why I spend so much time out at the sty when he comes back to Denton again. When the time is ripe, you'll all know." He pointed a fork at me. "You keep away from the pigpen, Lucinda. Don't you go sneaking out there, or I'll sic a sow on you."

I stuck out my tongue at him—the wicked pig doter!—and said, "I won't go near your pigs. Don't you worry. They don't smell at all good this summer. They never did. But I think they're worse now. They smell a little bit like that brown tonic. Sometimes I think that's what the breeze is bringing when I gather the eggs in the mornings."

He gave me a dreadful scowl and went back to his supper.

When the time is ripe! That seemed to me to be what just about everybody was saying these days.

On the twenty-fifth of August, Mama and Aunt Adelina and I boarded the train once more for Portland, to buy a wedding present for Gus and Eleanora, as well as to buy tonic ingredients.

I didn't go with them to the dry-goods stores to look at tablecloths. They let me go off on my own, window-shopping. When they were out of sight, though, instead of going into a confectionery store to buy horehound candy, I made a beeline for that little pharmacy on Jefferson Street. Here was my chance to satisfy my curiosity bump.

Breathless from running, I asked the man who stood behind the counter in front of shelves of shining-white apothecary jars, "Mister, do you know a lady from Denton called Mrs. Silas Westlake, who comes in here a lot?"

I had looked at his counter first and hadn't seen any bottles of the green wonder-worker on it, so I wasn't surprised when he didn't recognize my aunt's name. Maybe this shop was too small for the Apley twins to bother with.

The pharmacy man told me, "No, little girl, I don't know any lady by that name."

I went on. "She's smaller than I am and has dark hair with some gray in it and dark eyes that can bore holes through you when she wants them to. Some of the time she wears a gold lapel watch with diamonds in it."

He shook his head.

I said, "But I know you know her! I've seen her come in here several times."

All at once he yawned in my face as if he were sleepy; then he leaned his whiskery chin in one hand as he propped his elbow on his counter. "Why ask me if I know her when you seem to, little girl? What are you up to? Folks come in here and folks go out of here all the time. I don't talk to every customer enough to know him or her by name, you know. I can't help you, and even if I did know the lady personally by name, I wouldn't talk about her. I don't go around gabbing about my customers."

I said, "But all I want to know is what she comes in here to buy. I want to give some of it to her as a present, if I can afford it. Whatever she buys is very small because she puts it into her reticule."

He yawned again. "Now even if I was to tell you that I know the lady, I surely wouldn't tell you what she buys. I wouldn't tell that to anybody but the police, and they'd have to pry it out of me. What goes on between my customers and me is private business." Suddenly he opened his eyes wide and asked me, "Tell me, were *you* sent here by the police?"

"Of course not." I stepped back away from the counter.

It appeared to me that he wasn't about to tell me what I wanted to know, and it appeared, too, that he did know Aunt Adelina. But since I couldn't think of anything else to say to him, I turned around and marched right outside again. Thunderation, that had been a waste of time. Then another thought suddenly struck me.

I whirled about on the boardwalk and came back inside to ask, "Say, mister, are you the only one who ever clerks here?"

"Now that is something I *will* tell you. Yes. I am the sole owner and sole clerk. Good day to you, little girl."

That was that. If I wanted to know, it seemed I'd have to ask her myself, so that afternoon when we were on the train headed for home with the ingredients from the Second Street pharmacy and a purple-velvet table covering for the engaged couple, I asked, "Well, Aunt Adelina, while I was wandering around Portland, did you get what you wanted again at the little pharmacy on Jefferson Street?"

"Oh, I didn't go there this time, Lucinda. I have enough of the secret ingredient to last me for a long time." She was smiling as she watched Oregon passing by outside the window, not looking at me at all.

What had she meant by that? I was more mystified than ever.

When we got home that evening we found that something had happened in our absence. I knew what it was the moment I spotted Xerxes Apley sitting on our veranda top step with a very freckled, yellow-haired girl dressed in rose-colored calico.

I told Aunt Adelina, "I think it has to be Xenia."

"I fear so," said my aunt.

"Oh, dear," added Mama.

As we came through the gate, Xerxes got up and reached down to pull the girl up with him, too. "This is my sister Xenia," said Xerxes. "I guess you know about her coming, don't you?"

"We do. Your mother warned us about it," said my aunt.

"Does Xenia know about her new last name?" asked my mother.

"She knows she's supposed to pretend to be Xenia Howard until the time is ripe for her to be Xenia Apley again."

"Will you mind pretending to be Xenia Howard?" I asked the girl. She wasn't looking one bit pleased, and I couldn't blame her.

She scowled exactly the way Zenobia did, scrooching up her whole face. "You bet I mind it. It isn't right. I came all the way up to Denton on the stagecoach with some folks I knew who were bound for Portland. I thought I'd go to live in our house with Mama and the others. But when I got here yesterday, Mama told me that I have to live with you and pretend to be somebody else. So I came over with my brother Xerxes, who I don't hardly remember at all. Then Xerxes and the man and boy in this house tell me that they think it's all right if I call myself Xenia Howard. I think it's mighty odd. The two in there"—she jerked her thumb toward the house—"act very queer toward me. The man even snorted at me. Why would he do that?"

I said, "Oh, don't mind him, Xenia. He's doing that because this has happened before."

"Who to?" Xenia looked puzzled.

"It happened to me, Xenia," explained Xerxes. "I used to be Xerxes Westlake when I lived here. I didn't have the heart to tell you before you met the rest of the Howards and Westlakes. They're very nice people. They'll take good care of you."

"Yes, Xenia," said my aunt. "Silas has been warned this time so he won't blow up again."

"I don't understand what's happening," wailed the little girl from California.

Xerxes let out a sigh, then said good-bye to us, and, after kissing his sister on the cheek, left for home. Xenia sat down again, staring after him with a look on her face that made me think she might bawl at any minute. I brought out some lemonade and sat with her hoping she'd talk to me, but she wouldn't do anything but stare into the distance over the street.

Supper was strange that night. Now and then Uncle Silas looked across the table at Xenia as she picked at her supper. I supposed he had Mr. Heffer on his mind, too. Well, I was thinking about Heffer, but mostly about poor Xenia. I decided I'd be extra nice to her and try to put her at ease. It wasn't her fault her name was Apley.

After a while Xenia did open up a bit and become more friendly. She was lonesome and upset, but she liked to tramp around in the woods with me, gathering plants and roots. Doing that took my mind off what was looming in the future. The wedding day!

Both Victor and Willard came back to town on the first day of September. They brought tonic orders galore and cash, too. Oh, how those two strutted around town in those first few days, showing off their fancy striped and checkered suits and new fuzzy little moustaches. I watched the pair one day, sashaying past the Denton bank, leaning up against its front, lighting matches for their big cigars on the bricks. I saw how Banker Lambertson came out to greet them and

shake their hands. But they didn't spend much time with
him; he wasn't important enough for them. They went on
their way up the boardwalk, tipping their hats only to the
young, pretty ladies. Those awful Apley flirters! Why they
were both engaged. I was doubtful just how many women
they were betrothed to by now.

I followed behind them on their way to the Payday
Saloon to visit their stepfather-to-be. I was surely disgusted
by the way they acted, but being honest with myself, I had
to admit that part of my disgust could have come from
knowing that they'd gotten the shopkeepers in town to
start selling the green elixir when I'd failed. It was because
of them that Aunt Adelina was now getting some honor in
her hometown. I supposed I should be grateful to them for
that.

That same day I trailed the twins, I saw the Reverend
Curley and his wife coming toward me. This time, among
other things, I told them, "I hope you remember what I
said once about tonics that taste terrible. You both ought
to try my Aunt Adelina's elixir, which will soon be on sale
at the emporium and Quincy's and the pharmacy. It's green
in color and tastes nice and ferny like the woods."

"Is that so, Lucinda?" asked the minister.

"Oh, yes, it's so, all right. I am telling you the truth."

He changed the subject all at once from tonics to religion.
"Have you been reading the Bible lately, Lucinda?"

"Not too much. I've been working very hard helping out
my aunt and my uncle with the wonder-working tonic I told
you about, but I have looked into Ezekiel a couple of times
lately."

"I think you might like some other parts of the Good Book better, Lucinda."

"Oh, I don't know, sir. I thought Ezekiel was very exciting. Aren't you excited about marrying Mr. Heffer and Mrs. Apley in our parlor day after tomorrow, though?"

The tall minister leaned down to say, "I don't get excited at weddings anymore. I've married a great many people in my time. But it does please me to marry Mrs. Apley and Gus Heffer so they can share their remaining years together."

I told him, "Yes, that should be pleasant for you. Still I think this might be a more exciting wedding than you think. I sure hope it goes all right and Mr. Heffer doesn't decide to take the bit in his teeth and bolt."

"Bolt?" exclaimed Mrs. Curley.

"Yes, ma'am, that's just what I said. Good day to you." And I left them to go home, now that the Apley twins had gone inside the Payday. I had no wish to stay outside and wait for them to come out. I'd had my fill of Apleys for one day.

I had to admit to myself that I was very worried about the wedding-to-be. Mr. Heffer hadn't come over to our house, so he hadn't spotted Xenia. As far as any of us knew, Mrs. Apley hadn't told Mr. Heffer about her yet. Aunt Adelina had asked her straight out three times, and each time Mrs. Apley had smiled and told her, "It's all right. Don't you fret about it."

We were all fretting, though. Time was getting short, and Xenia was still with us. She didn't like it, and neither did we.

Mama and Aunt Adelina and I spent the morning of the

wedding draping our swept-and-dusted parlor with white bunting and filling vases with bunches of white syringa and pink and white roses to make it look bridal.

Mrs. Apley came at noon and went upstairs with Mama to change into her wedding gown and get Zenobia and Yolanda into the proper frame of mind to be wedding attendants. They hadn't brought any flowers with them, so I got four big calla lilies out of the fireplace scuttle and went upstairs with them.

On the way up, I had to step carefully around Xerxes and Xenia sitting side by side on the bottom step of the landing. Xerxes was wearing a new suit of dark-gray serge, which became him, but thunderation, his sister was going to be noticed at the ceremony! I don't know where in Portland Mrs. Apley had gotten hold of the cloth, but poor Xenia had on a gown of bright, parrot-green taffeta with a real bustle at the back, even though she was too young to wear a bustle. She had on high-heeled, white boots with pearl buttons and a dark-green bonnet with white plumes and red roses. I thought she looked miserable sitting there with her hands clamped tight on her green knees, which were probably shaking.

I laid two of the calla lilies over her hands and said, not too truthfully, "My, but you do look pretty, Xenia, and so grown up, too."

"No, I don't look pretty neither, Lucinda. I looked at myself in your mirror before I came out here with my brother. I'm suffering. Mama made me wear a corset, and it's cutting me in half. I can't hardly get my breath she laced me in so tight. If I'd knowed it was going to be so bad up here in Oregon, I would've stayed down in Grass Valley. I wish I was back there now."

"There, there, Xenia. It'll all be over soon," said Xerxes. Then he added under his breath, "I hope it will anyhow."

I sighed and went on my way to Aunt Adelina's bedroom and rapped on the door. Mama was fixing the hooks and eyes on the back of Mrs. Apley's peach-colored wedding dress, while Aunt Adelina arranged the creamy lace on the polonaise so it would drape right. Mrs. Apley looked very elegant today, I thought. The pearl-and-diamond earrings Mr. Heffer had given her as a wedding present sparkled under her just-hennaed hair.

Yolanda and Zenobia, who were dressed in pale-green frocks with parrot-green taffeta sashes the color of Xenia's gown, sat on the bed stiff as statues, to keep from getting their dresses wrinkled. I went over to them and stuffed a calla lily into the clasped hand of each little girl. Then I went to Aunt Adelina's night table to sniff the bridal bouquet of baby's breath, ferns, and yellow rosebuds.

Mama joined me there after she'd finished with Mrs. Apley, and I asked her very softly, "Has Mrs. Apley said yet whether Mr. Heffer knows about Xenia? What's she said to you so far this afternoon?"

"She's talked about a number of things—about their honeymoon up in Portland and the elixir and Victor and Willard doing so well and Xerxes going to Denton Academy and how well behaved the little girls are today, but not one word so far about Xenia."

"Oh, Mama, have you seen Xenia yet? She's sitting outside on the steps."

"Yes, I saw her. That poor child. She should be dressed like her little sisters, not like a grown-up lady. I think Eleanora wants Mr. Heffer to get the idea that Xenia is older than she is and will soon be out on her own." Mama looked at me in what I thought was a rather sad way. "You know, you and your brother are growing up on me, both of you. You'll be putting your hair up on top of your head and your skirts down to your ankles at the end of this month when you start Denton Academy. You won't ever again wear that pretty white-muslin frock you're wearing now. And you'll have to go into corsets at the middle of this month."

I spoke my piece now, though I supposed I might have picked a better time for it. "No, Mama, I don't want to do that. I've had a lot of time to think things over since Caralee and I aren't best friends anymore. If Aunt Adelina won't wear corsets, I won't either. I admire her a lot more than I admire Caralee. I don't want to faint away because I can't get my breath the way Caralee's mother does sometimes. Mama, do I have to wear those danged contraptions? I don't care if my waist is bigger than Caralee's or even her mother's."

"No, Lucinda." Mama hesitated for a moment, then went on. "Corsets really are not healthful. In fact, they're downright dangerous. I think I'll give up mine, too, and breathe the way a person should. Let people think that I'm odd. I don't care anymore what Denton people think of me." She pinched my cheek gently, smiling. "After all, we are considered quite queer here. Your aunt's success in business and her spirit friends, like Mr. Whitlow, have seen to that."

I looked around me to make sure nobody was listening to

us and whispered, "Oh, Mama, if I'm to start Denton Academy in two weeks, don't you think I'm old enough now to know about *him*?"

"Him? Who, Lucinda?"

I hissed, "Mr. Whitlow!"

She laughed softly. "I suppose you are at that. You've been through a lot of dismaying things this year, and you've held up just fine. So you have a right to know. He was the skeleton in the family closet back home in Pennsylvania—a great-great-great uncle on your grandfather's side of the family. Adelina says Whitlow returned as her guardian and advisor because he wants to help make up for the wicked life he led on earth. He was certainly no angel here."

"Mama, *what* was he?"

"A pirate, my dear. A real live pirate. Second mate under the dreadful Blackbeard, Captain Teach. According to your aunt, Mr. Whitlow disagreed once with Blackbeard when both of them were drunk, and Blackbeard made him walk the plank of the pirate ship into the Atlantic Ocean. He was drowned."

Thunderation! A pirate ancestor. I was thrilled all the way down to the tassels on my best black-kid boots.

Mama might have gone on thrilling me, but at that moment there was a yelling sound from below. I went to the bedroom window and leaned out. One of the twins—was it Victor or was it Willard?—was driving the shiny new black rig Mr. Heffer had bought, and the other was sitting next to him. Mr. Heffer, elegant in a fawn-brown Prince Albert coat and a high silk hat and cream-colored trousers, was seated in the back next to the black-coated Reverend Curley.

Oh, but I had butterflies in my stomach as the four men got out of the carriage and one of the twins tethered Heffer's frisky white horse to our gatepost.

I turned around and told everyone, "They're here. Uncle Silas'll be letting them in below now."

Mama said, "It's time for me to go down to the cottage organ." She hurried over to Mrs. Apley and kissed her on the cheek. "You are a beautiful bride, my dear. I hope that everything is in readiness for your wedding."

"Oh, I'm so flustered," cried Mrs. Apley. "I've been up in the air for days and hardly know what I'm doing anymore."

I caught the eye of my aunt and didn't like what I saw there. I read her mind at that moment and I think she read mine, but all she said was, "Please, Lucinda, get Xerxes and Xenia in here now."

I opened the door and called them, and they filed sadly inside. Then I hurried downstairs with Aunt Adelina to the parlor where everybody had assembled.

Just outside the portieres, I collided with Henry Frederick, who hissed at me, "Lucinda, did Mrs. Apley 'fess up yet about Xenia to Heffer?"

I hissed back, "I don't know, but I sure hope so. Come on. She'll be on her way downstairs any minute now. Can't you hear Mama playing the wedding march?"

He and I went into the parlor together and squeezed ourselves into the space in front of the bookcase. Our parlor was full of folks already—Apleys and Howards and Westlakes— and the preacher and Mr. Heffer were standing next to the lily-filled fireplace.

The creaking sounds on the stairs told us that they were coming down. I held my breath and crossed my fingers behind my back.

First came Zenobia and Yolanda, looking very serious and important, holding the calla lilies straight up like spears. Then came Xenia, walking alone and clutching her flowers the proper way. I thought she looked very worried, and I saw she was having trouble with her high-heeled boots because she was wobbling.

Last came a smiling Mrs. Apley, with one hand on the arm of Xerxes, who looked more miserable than I'd ever seen him. He caught my eye and gave just the tiniest shake of his head.

I gasped at his warning signal. *She hadn't told him!*

Alas, we could tell that Mr. Heffer knew at once Xenia was a relation. First he stared at her; then he glared at Mrs. Apley. Finally he pointed and said very loudly, "Eleanora, who is that yellow-headed girl? Is that another *Apley?*"

"Oh, Gus!" I saw Mrs. Apley's face start to fall and her nosegay begin to tremble. "She's my Xenia, my oldest girl child. I wanted to tell you before, but I was scared to."

Heffer turned and roared at my uncle, "Si, did you know about this?"

"I'm afraid so, Gus. I'm sorry."

"Well, Si, if you know, so does everybody else around here." Mr. Heffer turned his head toward the minister. "I take it you knew about this here gal, too, Mr. Curley?"

"No, Mr. Heffer, I didn't." I thought the minister seemed upset, and I nodded at him but he wasn't looking at me. He put his hand on Heffer's arm and said, "Don't bolt, Gus.

I'm sure we can straighten this out and go on with the ceremony."

"No, I don't know that I plan to, Mr. Curley. I promised fair and square to marry this widow lady here, and I took on three of her offspring when we started courting. But she's gone and rung in three more on me since that time. I wonder how many others she's got stuck out in the woods someplace. There's a whole flock of them, it seems to me. Eleanora, is this here gal maybe half of another pair of twins?"

"Oh, no, Gus. She's all there is of us now," wailed Mrs. Apley. "Gus, we ain't poor no more. We can support Xenia, too, can't we? She don't eat a lot. Look how skinny she is. I can support her all by myself if I have to, if that's the way you want it."

"I want to go back to California," cried Xenia, as tears rolled down her cheeks. But nobody was listening or looking at her but me.

Mr. Heffer told her mother, "It ain't the money, Eleanora. It's your confounded scheming. Can I ever believe anything you tell me now, or am I going to have to wonder all the rest of my life about what you maybe *ain't* telling me? Will there be more and more Apleys popping up out of nowhere all the time?"

"No, Gus, there won't be. I'll swear to that on the Bible. Xenia is the last of the lot. All I ever had in the way of kids was from *V* to *Z*, with two *X*'s."

He said grimly, "But there's *A* to *U* that comes before *V*."

I couldn't move a muscle if I wanted to. This wedding was like a melodrama on the stage of the theater on Spruce Street, but this time I was in the play, not just watching it from a nice peaceful seat.

All at once Xerxes spoke up, "Mr. Heffer, Xenia is really and truly all there is of us Apleys. Mother won't deceive you anymore ever. She can't."

This calmed Heffer down a good bit. He mumbled, "All right, Xerxes. I'll believe you because I know your nature. But I'm not one bit happy about this latest game. This new gal is a danged queer bridegroom present for any man to get from his loving bride. Frankly, I'm not eager now to go on with tieing this knot."

"I want to go home to Grass Valley," Xenia put in, but once more nobody was paying any heed to her.

Aunt Adelina was the one everyone was looking at. She'd gone to the cottage organ and, reaching past Mama's shoulder, had played one loud chord to get everybody's attention. Her voice rang out briskly, "I had foreseen this. I think that I had best do what I can now to make this situation a bit sweeter for everyone. The time is ripe." She went up to Mrs. Apley's side, stood on her tiptoes, and spoke for just an instant into Mrs. Apley's right ear, cupping her hand against it so that no one would hear what she'd said.

"Why, Missus Westlake!" cried the bride.

"That's right, Eleanora. Now you and I are the only two persons in the world who know the secret ingredient of my green elixir, and you are sworn to complete secrecy about it." My aunt spoke to Mr. Heffer next. "Gus, it appears to me that Eleanora should be a more desirable and precious partner to you than ever before. Can you afford to let this magnificent motherly lady go out of your life forever? If she loves her children so much, think of how she will love you!"

For a while Mr. Heffer teetered on the heels of his boots, then finally he muttered, "She was precious to me from the start, Mrs. Westlake. I guess Eleanora still is in spite of all her kids, and since this new one's another gal and not a boy, I'll go along with it. But this better be the last one, gal or no gal. I won't stand for another one."

"Oh, Gus!" the bride cried and flung her arms around him.

"Shall we continue the wedding then?" asked Mr. Curley, whose hands seemed to be white around the knuckles as they held the prayer book.

"Let's go. I suppose we might as well get it over with," agreed Heffer. "Come on, Xerxes, hand your mama over to me."

Xerxes spoke straight out, while all the grown-ups stared at him, nervous that his words would stop the wedding again. "Mr. Heffer, are you going to welcome Xenia or not?"

"Yes, I will," Heffer said. Then he looked at Xenia and asked, "How old are you?"

"Going on twelve, sir."

He sniffed. "You're duded up to look thirty years old. Once this is over, you get back in clothes that suit a gal your age, you hear me, and quit bawling. I won't eat you!"

"Yes, sir, I hear you."

"Come on, Xerxes, do your duty," ordered Mr. Heffer. "Hand your mama over now."

I watched Xenia's face as the ceremony went on. She wasn't exactly smiling the way Xerxes and Mrs. Apley and the little girls were, but she wasn't bawling either, even if she was gripping the calla lilies so hard that their stalks were breaking.

After the ceremony was over and everybody was milling around kissing the bride and shaking Mr. Heffer's hand, I talked to Xerxes and Xenia for a while. I asked him, "Are there truly only six of you Apleys?"

Xerxes nodded. "Yes, Lucinda, unless Mother and Mr. Heffer have some of their own, and they'll be only half Apley. Mother surely takes to the idea of having a family. She dotes on babies."

Xenia said, "Yes, she does. Lucinda, I'm going to go up and get back into my calico dress, but you stay down here. I think I can get out of the corsets alone." She gave me a smile and left.

Once she was gone I went over to the newlyweds and told them that I hoped they would be very happy together. Eleanora Heffer couldn't take her gaze off her new husband. She should have swatted Yolanda and Zenobia, who were running up and down the hallway, shrieking and hitting each other over the head with the lilies, but she didn't.

They carried on like that while we ate wedding cake in the dining room, and they were still running about when Xenia came down the steps in her rose-colored calico dress. I called out to her to come have some cake, too, but she paid no attention to me. Instead she went and grabbed Zenobia and Yolanda, who were gliding up and down the polished floor on a braided rug, and shook them. I thought she was doing a fine thing and felt like clapping.

Well, sir, I wasn't alone in that feeling because that was exactly what somebody behind me was doing. Aunt Adelina and Mr. Heffer were both clapping.

I heard him say to her, "That oldest Apley gal seems to have some good qualities in her, wouldn't you say, Mrs. Westlake?"

"Indeed, I do, Mr. Heffer. We are sorry to have deceived

you about her, but we have grown very fond of Xenia in the short time we've known her. She has a good, sensible head, and I think she'll give you no trouble at all."

"She acts older'n eleven, huh?"

"Much older than that. She's worth educating, too, and there'll be money for that."

"I reckon, Mrs. Westlake, that by this time next year there'll be so much money coming in that I'll give up the saloon business for the tonic business. The only alcohol I'll deal with will go into the elixir."

"That's very good news, Gus," were her final words before Uncle Silas called her back into the dining room.

The Heffers had their wedding supper at the Denton Hotel. It was a fine supper of roast beef and turkey and champagne. I had a half glass of champagne, but decided that I preferred dandelion wine.

At the end of the meal, Victor stood up and said, "I have an announcement to make now before Ma and Gus go off on their honeymoon. Mrs. Westlake has been good as gold to us Apleys all along, and today she's even given Ma a great big wedding present, the name of the secret ingredient of the wonder-working elixir that me and Willard are selling hand over fist. We tried to find out what it was from Ma right after the ceremony, but the bride won't even tell her own sons. She says it's her little trade secret."

Everybody laughed to hear this, but most of all Victor, who'd made the joke and shouldn't have laughed.

Aunt Adelina told Eleanora, "And don't you ever tell him or anyone else in your family. Keep it our trade secret. Always tell people who ask you that the ingredients in the green tonic are 'just some weeds from the wilderness.'"

"I won't tell Victor or anybody else, I promise you. Not even my dearly beloved sweet Gus. I won't even whisper it in my sleep."

Victor, who was still standing up, went on now. "Well, I've got a secret of my own, folks. Willard and me and Henry Fred have a present for you, Mrs. Westlake."

"You have?" My aunt looked surprised, and so did everybody else.

He said, "You bet we have. It's about a hair restorer."

Aunt Adelina asked in the sudden quiet that had fallen over the table, "My Hopi Hair Restorer? What about it, Victor?"

"Oh, that ain't the one we mean, Mrs. Westlake," said Willard, who was sitting across the table from his brother.

"But that's the only one there is!" exclaimed Mama.

"No, it isn't!" Henry Frederick burst in now. "The tonic number one, the brown one that smelled so bad, is the one we're talking about."

"You mean the one that failed, Henry Frederick?" asked Aunt Adelina.

I pointed at my brother. "The one you've been giving to our pigs and the Apley pigs, the one that's making them bulk up and get ferocious?"

He bobbed his head up and down and grinned. "That's the one." All at once he jumped up out of his chair and cried, "But the pigs aren't just bulking up. There's more. We've got the bristliest, hairiest pigs in Denton, probably the hairiest pigs in the whole United States. The piglets look more like puppies than porkers. That's why we wanted everybody to keep away from the pigpens lately. The pigs aren't any more ferocious than pigs anywhere else, but they're sure different. We didn't want folks to see them and start talking around town." He sat down, still grinning.

"Victor, is this true?" asked Uncle Silas.

"Is it a true fact?" said Mr. Heffer, who was passing his hand over his balding head and frowning.

"Yes, it's a fact. They permitted me to see the animals," Xerxes put in quietly.

"Good gracious, this is most remarkable." I saw how Aunt Adelina was staring into the flames of the hotel candelabra on the table in front of her. "Oh, I do hope I can recall that formula again. I threw away the papers I'd jotted it down on because I thought it was good for nothing, and now I find that it's good for something after all. It might have some possibilities for human beings."

"Please try to bring it back to mind, Mrs. Westlake," urged Mr. Heffer. "If it works on beasts, it might work on men."

"Gus, I shall try. If I succeed, I think I might donate the very first bottle to a worthy cause here in Denton." I heard her chuckle.

"Well, Adelina, that worthy cause ought to be the top of my head. I'll gladly test it out for you," answered Heffer.

"No, Gus, what I meant was Mr. Lambertson's head." She added, "I can remember all too well what the tonic smelled and tasted like. I wonder what our pork will taste like—not like the tonic, I sincerely hope."

"Aunt Adelina," I said, "those pigs smell just like it. Even from the chicken coop I can smell it. I don't think—"

My brother burst in rudely on me. "That's right. You

don't think, Lucinda. You shouldn't ever eat those pigs. They're special sights to be seen. They're pioneers and trade secrets, too."

Xerxes said now, "He's quite right, you know. It would be very unkind to eat them after all they might be doing for you, Mrs. Westlake."

"All right, all right, boys," said Uncle Silas, shaking his head and smiling. "Adelina, if you can recall and write down the recipe for that brown stuff, I think you might consider giving the formula to our Howard children and to Victor and Willard and the rest of the Apley kids. Your green wonder-worker is going to be plenty profitable for us grown-ups."

I saw how her hand went out over Uncle Silas's on the tabletop. "I'll do that if I can bring it back to mind, Silas."

"Hurray!" shouted my brother, annoying other dining-room customers, who turned around and glared at us. "Then we won't be poor relations anymore!"

"If that tonic can do what I think it can do, you sure won't be poor, Henry Fred, and you neither, Lucy," said Victor, nearly as loudly as my brother.

"No, indeed," agreed Uncle Silas more quietly. "We are going to be *your* poor relations if that brown tonic can really grow hair on a man's scalp." He looked at Aunt Adelina. "Well, Adelina, will you be on the label of that, too? I guess it'd be your right."

For a long moment there was complete quiet; then she said, "No, Silas, you will be—if you'd like."

Like everybody else, I got to bed late that night, after helping Xenia pack her carpetbags so she could move back to her mother's house. Because of all the excitement I couldn't sleep. I lay propped up on pillows, watching the moonlight creep along my quilt toward my face as the moon rose higher in the sky. I thought about all the remarkable things that had happened in 1874—our recovering from being ruined, the burglary, all of the Apleys, the unusual wedding today, and of the pigs growing hair.

That report about the pigs had been true, all right. When we got home from the Denton Hotel, we Howards and Westlakes had lit lanterns and gone out to our sty to look at our pigs. They were very hairy pigs, indeed, and friendly like spaniels, not ferocious at all.

Then I thought of my trip to the pharmacy on Jefferson Street in Portland and of the secret ingredient of the green wonder-worker. *What could it be?* Twirling one of my braids of hair around on a finger, I thought of what a very brief time my aunt spent in there and of the briefer time she'd spent whispering into Mrs. Apley's ear.

Whatever the secret ingredient was, it had to be tiny to be carried in such a little reticule, and its name had to be short enough to be said quickly. Thunderation, could her going in the pharmacy have been only a trick of sorts? A trade secret. That must be what it was.

All at once I thought I understood her doings and because of them I admired Adelina Westlake more than ever. She'd come up with some hocus-pocus to fool even me and Mrs. Apley.

A bright light flared up in my head. It wasn't an herb or a root or a weed from the wilderness at all! It wasn't even anything to carry in a reticule or lock up in a cedar chest.

I spoke out loud to the moonlight. "I think it's a word, just a word, and probably only *one* word. And I'll bet that word is *hope*. A pinch of hope? That's what she puts into the pots of tonic. That's what she needed most to start out in business with—hope!"

And then it happened. *It happened to me!* There came such a loud thudding sound on one of the walls of my bedroom that I nearly fell out of bed with astonishment. The next second two of the three pictures on the wall fell crashing down together onto the carpet.

Him? Here?

Answering *me*, Lucinda Lavina Howard?

Shivering all over with the willies, I pulled the quilt up to my chin and said to the wall, "No, I won't ever tell anyone what it is—most of all Aunt Adelina. But it is hope, isn't it?"

Now the third and last picture fell off its nail down to the carpet.

I let out a small yelping sound, then jerked the quilt and sheets up over my head. It seemed that I had that old pirate as a guardian spirit, too. Thunderation, he must run in the family!

I whispered as politely as I could to the bedcovers shaking over my head, "Thank you, thank you, Mr. Whitlow, sir."

Author's Note

Young readers may not be familiar with that legendary nine-teenth-century businesswoman and advertising pioneer, Lydia E. Pinkham. Adults, however, may remember seeing bottles of her renowned "Vegetable Compound" in their homes as children.

Mrs. Pinkham was quite a remarkable woman for her day. She was an American pioneer in many ways, although she lived in Massachusetts, not in Oregon's Willamette Valley, where I've placed my fictional Adelina Westlake, who is modeled after Lydia Pinkham.

Mr. Pinkham was much like Silas Westlake, an amiable but not very successful businessman, a jack-of-all-trades, who had enjoyed varied fortunes and, like Uncle Silas, co-signed bank notes for his friends. Mr. Pinkham was ruined in the Panic of 1873, and as partial payment for a friend's debt he was given the formula for the compound that was to make his wife famous.

This formula, though, didn't have an Indian name. In the book I've called the elixir the Tuscarora Tonic because so many patent medicines of the nineteenth century had Indian names.

Mrs. Pinkham's enterprising sons sold the tonic, and it was one of her sons who conceived the idea of featuring her likeness on the bottle label, thereby revolutionizing advertising of the time.

No respectable woman would have allowed her image to appear in such a way. Moreover, women didn't go into business for themselves. Unlike Aunt Adelina, Mrs. Pinkham struggled long to become established, but at the time of her death, in 1883, she had built up a $300,000-a-year business and was spending $18,000 for advertising.

The fact that the solvent for the Pinkham tonic was alcohol disturbed some men of that time who were afraid that their wives might become alcoholics by taking the elixir at home. In order to negate the charge that her tonic made "topers out of ladies," Lydia Pinkham's company (which, by the way, is still in business) made the tonic available to a group of confirmed alcoholics in Boston. In all cases these hardened drinkers got sick on the tonic before they could get drunk on it.

As a result of the success of her vegetable compound, Lydia became a social worker and an advice giver of sorts, replying by mail to people who wrote her because they felt they knew her through her tonic. Like Adelina Westlake, Pinkham was both a champion of women's rights and a spiritualist, as well as a supporter of decent and healthful working conditions for women workers in the 1880's. It took enormous courage for a woman to hold any of these convictions then.

In writing of the various products my fictional characters concoct, I've tried to use actual formulas from the last century, although I've given the preparations some fanciful names of my own. The lead-and-sulphur hair restorer was a real product, and so are the formulas for the hand cream, face powder, and wrinkle cream. The gin-and-water treatment was an actual remedy used during Civil War days for red faces.

The list of herbs and roots I included in the Tuscarora Tonic were and still are used by herbalists. The Oregon substitutes were taught to the pioneer women by the Indians. The roots of Oregon grape, wild licorice, and poppy were used in tonics made in the state a hundred years ago.

I've also spoken of some special dishes that actually appeared on dinner tables in old Oregon, such as apple grunt, sea-clam jam, and fern pie.

I've described Portland as it was in the 1870's, the metropolis of the new state. Denton does not exist, but Oregon readers will probably recognize it as a prototype of the neat, pretty cities of the green Willamette Valley in pioneer days.

Even though it may sound unbelievable that Lucinda's family would have to pay for her high-school education, this was common practice in the 1870's. High schools were not public schools in those days, and going to high school was a privilege not extended to all young people, as only the better students were admitted.

I have tried to explain a few of the causes of the Panic of 1873, as well as some of the procedures involved in banking and in setting up a business. I wish to express my gratitude to my economist-husband, Professor Carl G. Uhr of the University of California, Riverside, for his help in this regard.

I also wish to extend my thanks to Marcia Goerbe, Librarian of the Literature and History Department of the Portland, Oregon Library Association and a gracious member of the Monterey Park, California Library Board, Peggy Perry, who suggested that I use the name of her great grandmother in one of my novels someday. That ancestress was Lucinda Lavina Howard.

Patricia Beatty
April 1977

About the Author

Now a resident of Southern California, Patricia Beatty was born in Portland, Oregon. She was graduated from Reed College there, and then taught high-school English and history for four years. Later she held various positions as science and technical librarian and also as a children's librarian. Quite recently she has taught Writing Fiction for Children in the Extension Department of the University of California, Los Angeles. She has had a number of historical novels published by Morrow, several of them dealing with the American West in the 1860 to 1895 period.

With her late husband, Dr. John Beatty, Mrs. Beatty also coauthored a number of books. One of them, *The Royal Dirk*, was chosen as an Award Book by the Southern California Council on Children's and Young People's Literature. Subsequently Mrs. Beatty received another award from the Council for her Distinguished Body of Work.

Mrs. Beatty is now married to a professor of economics at the University of California, Riverside, and she has a married daughter, Alexandra Beatty Stewart.